London Decamerone

History in short stories

Herstellung und Verlag:
BoD – Books on Demand, Norderstedt
Copyright: 2017 Karl Heinz Landenberger
ISBN 978-3-7460-5638-8

A day in London

I like London (1.1)

It is a city where history is ever present, unlike any other city.

On the very first day of my stay, I took a walk in Hyde Park. I started off at Lancaster Gate, close to where I had rented an appartement. London parks are a highlight for me. The lush green grass – lush because of the humid climate – is something I had only ever seen in pre-alpine landscapes until then. The park was filled to the brim with joggers and athletic female runners. Almost all of them were running with bare legs even though it was already late fall, however, temperatures were still mild.

Londoners love dogs. They will walk up to six dogs at once, three on each hand. Still, there was no dog dirt to be found – that is how disciplined Englishmen are. Quite the contrary in France, by the way. On the Côte d'azur in Southern France, you will step from one pile into the other even in the most renowned of holiday resorts.

The leaves were still hanging on the trees, many bushes were blooming and wild cyclamens were growing around their edges. I passed the magnificent Italian parks and charmingly arranged lakes to finally end up at Speaker's Corner. I should have become a photographer, just so I could capture all these beautiful sights and publish them as "Impressions of London." Everything I had seen on TV so far didn't match up to the – actual – magnificence that I beheld there.

Speaker's Corner

I noticed him right away. He was standing with a small group of people who were watching a man with tattoos all over his body. This man was gradually undressing himself to show off every last tattoo and to explain their meaning while yelling: "I'm a human being" again and again, even though no one was questioning that fact.

Apparently, I had also in turn caught the attention of the spectator I had noticed because he came to me and addressed me directly. He didn't open with "Where are you from" or "What's your name," instead, he wanted to get my opinion on the speaker's performance. Well, to be honest, I am not a big fan of tattoos. I just don't understand how someone can disfigure their own body like that. About the performance and statements themselves, I had nothing much to say. The tattoo-enthusiast was talking about the four freedoms humans should have according to US president Franklin Delano Roosevelt, the same freedoms American soldiers fought for in World War II.

Bohemians of Bigger London

The then still unfamiliar man who had approached me knew more than I did and was able to tell me that the tattoos had been etched into the performer's skin based on sketches by the American painter Norman Rockwell. He also told me that the tattoed man had been doing this same performance for years and that he knew him personally. Both belonged to a loosely knitted group of "Bohemians of Bigger London," who sometimes also worked together and organized shows and events in cafes or pubs.

My new acquaintance's role mostly consisted of telling stories, anecdotes, jokes, and, most of all, weird stories. He was quite the linguist, a polyglot, and able to tell his stories in almost any language. His nickname therefore was "Tusitala – Teller of a thousand stories," a name the Samoans had once given the author of Treasure Island, who spent his twilight years in Samoa.

Hyde Park

While talking, we wandered along the shores of the serpentine lake and passed Albert Memorial. We went by the wonderful Kensington Palace where Queen Victoria had once resided, a queen who had lent her name to an entire era, and walked past the Princess Diana Memorial. We also took a look at the fanciful Peter Pan statue and finally wound up at my point of origin, the Lancaster Gate. We were so engrossed in our conversation that we kept on walking and in the end, we found ourselves at Speaker's Corner once again.

Political conversations (1.2)

Freedom from fear

Our conversation centered around the four freedoms. Freedom of speech, freedom of worship, freedom from want, and the fourth one, freedom from fear. This fourth freedom was a promise the American president made, promising all of humanity that he would create a world without fear as soon as peace was restored after World War II. He promised the world this Pax Americana at a time when the USA had not even entered the war yet. It was a promise to never have another war, to have eternal peace instead as soon as Hitler was taken care of – world peace under American leadership. In order to achieve this, however, the USA first had to enter the war.

Entering the war

Churchill could hardly wait for that moment to come because England had no chance of continuing the war without American support after its defeat at Dunkirk and France's surrender. The American public however had no wish to be drawn into yet another World War, the same as with World War I. Still, Churchill knew that England wouldn't be able to win a European war, only a World War, side by side with the United States. Roosevelt had already promised him in 1932, we're going to destroy Germany and do it right this time.

Norman Rockwell

The American painter has created an enigmatic picture to visualize this fourth freedom. The tattoo-guy was carrying it on his chest, the most prominent place so to speak. A small boy and his sister are lying next to each other in their sickbed. Father and mother are standing close to them and are worried about their sleeping children.

Interpretation

The worried parents are the world powers Uncle Sam and Britannia. But just as the two children can put all their trust in them, so can the world. The global community does not have to fear these two world powers. They will protect all peoples and foster them. To do this, however, they will first have to take their weapons so they can't wage war against one another. A world without weapons is a world where no one can start a war, a world where well-being and prosperity are guaranteed by the US and the UK, and them alone. This disarmament would hit Germany first. „Never again will a German hold a weapon in their hands". After this, Japan would also have to surrender unconditionally and forego any kind of weaponization.

Step by step, all other countries would have to be demilitarized as well.

UN – Charta

This thought was also expressed in the UN – Charta that was devised by Churchill and Roosevelt in 1941. They met in absolute secrecy on the British battleship HMS Prince of Wales in Placenta Bay in front of Newfoundland from the 9th-12th of August 1941. Shortly before that, Hitler had invaded the Soviet Union and both politicians assumed that Hitler would win. They thought they could then easily destroy the weakened German army, especially since the most enormous weaponry a country had ever built, and that Roosevelt had started to have built in 1932, would be ready for combat in 1942, following the "10-year rule." Article 8 states: We are convinced that it is necessary for all peoples of this world to renounce the use of any armed force for practical and moral reasons. Peace cannot be maintained permanently as long as assault weapons can be used to attack others. That is why we find that in order to create a permanent system of general security, it is necessary that all nations be demilitarized. With this, we support any measures aimed at relieving peace-loving peoples of the pressure to get armed.

Unpolitical

All I could do was listen to my new friend, Houston. He told me so many new things. I myself had been brought up apolitically as was my whole generation. I only knew there would never be another war after Hitler had been defeated. I was convinced of that. It was absolutely inconceivable that there could be another maniac like that out there that would be able to pull the world into such an extermination war as Hitler had done. Hitler was the only one of his kind, that was clear to everybody. All of my classmates thought so and my teachers said the same thing.

The fact that the Americans were willing to protect us selflessly and take all of the weight of armament on themselves – I thought that was very altruistic of them. I shared my opinions with my new friend, who didn't quite agree with me. Today, I don't agree either anymore. "No more wars" was an empty promise made by the victors. The only thing they did with this was conceal their claims to world domination.

Dreams meet reality

Furthermore, the war did not at all turn out as Churchill and Roosevelt had imagined. Bolshevism wasn't destroyed; instead, Stalin came out of the war stronger than ever, you could even say he won it. His army was the one to invade Berlin, not the US or British army. He occupied the capital's city center and voluntarily gave the other victors only a few sectors in the Western part of the city.

In the Pacific, Chiang Kai-shek didn't defeat the Japanese, the US had to personally intervene in order to beat Japan. The generalissimo even lost mainland China, which Mao Tse Tung, Stalin's new ally, conquered in a "Long March." Hence, Bolshevism was also established in the East. The only thing left to nationalist China was the small island of Taiwan, the former Formosa.
Two new world powers were created by the war. The US and the UK had to share world domination with them. They had to

grant the same UN veto rights to both of them. It was no longer two countries that had last say, now it was four. That means that the struggle for domination was still on-going – eternal peace, yeah, right.

The only thing the war resulted in was the total destruction of Germany and Japan.

Operation Unthinkable

Churchill realized: „We killed the wrong pig." He wanted to continue the war one day after the peace agreement in May of 1945. He had the weapons of the more than 5 million imprisoned German soldiers collected. They were supposed to be given back to them so that they could continue the war against the Russians side by side with American and British soldiers. However, the US generals just didn't cooperate. The landing in Normandy and battles in the West had been more difficult and cost more lives than expected, in spite of their enormous material superiority. They weren't able to continue the war like that without a break. The only possible war was the Cold War – unlike the situation in the East.

One war after the other

The war in the Pacific region had started in Korea, where in 1936, the USA had provided Chiang Kai-shek with money and arms for his fight against Japan. And that is where the war continued right away. When the USA wanted to occupy these rich colonies after the Japanese had been banished, the Koreans resisted. The Korean people paid a high price for the American military maneuvers. 3 million people lost their lives, all of them were Korean. To this day, North Korea has not been conquered. The only thing they have there is a truce that could be broken at any time. The situation is especially precarious at the moment.

After this came the Vietnam War. Vietnam didn't want to allow the French colonial power to reinstate its dominance. The USA wanted to use this so they could assert their dominance over Vietnam. But even though the USA were using extremely cruel measures such as throwing napalm bombs, they didn't manage to win this war.

The intervention in Iran, the war on Saddam Hussein in Iraq, Serbia, the war on Gaddafi in Libya, giving weapons to oppositionists in Syria so a civil war would ensue and more than 1,200 military interventions – the USA are involved in all of that. So that's the result of their promise of a world without fear, this is their realization of peace eternal.
One could quote Brecht and say, "The dream of peace is no longer a dream, it has become a harsh reality."

Côte d'azur (1.3)

Memories

These conversations brought us very close together in a remarkably short time. I also learned much about his family, his childhood and adolescence. I learned that he went against his parents' wishes early on and chose a path that went against the family tradition. He didn't study at Oxford and climb the career ladder afterwards; instead, he first lived as a vagabond, a globetrotter and after that, as a freelance writer. As an adolescent, he liked to camp on the French Mediterranean coast with his friends. That brought up memories for both of us. We remembered that we had actually met once before, on the beach in front of the Negresco in Nice just a few years after the Second World War.

Back then, the beach was still covered in pebbles. It was only later that sand was heaped onto it. Today, all hotels and restaurants belong to rich oil sheiks. He was with his friends, the beautiful Cynthia, Douglas and Charles. His first name was Houston. Back then, I went by Henry and was added to this four-leaf clover. I was 16, 2 years younger than my new friends, and I was seriously considering breaking out of my bourgeois home to roam across the world with those four Londoners.

Educated middle-class

My parents, always eager to learn, visited the house of famous impressionist Auguste Renoir and the Grimaldi Palace in Antibes. This is where Picasso had painted his famous picture "La Joie de vivre." They also went to other places where renowned painters had worked and would not miss a single famous museum or studio of the great painters. The South of France was an artist's paradise, especially after 1945, but even long before that, van Gogh and Gauguin were living in Arles in the Provence.

Street artists

My four friends weren't interested in the works of others, they were artists themselves. Charles created wonderful street pictures on the sidewalk. Usually they were caricatures of living great politicians. General de Gaulle with a huge nose or Churchill, the Little Fat Man with a cigar. In appreciation, the people strolling along the shore promenade would throw coins into the cap lying next to the pictures.

Cynthia was able to draw astonishingly good portraits with just a few strokes. She would set up her small, wobbly easel and hardly any passersby were able to resist buying the sketch. Everybody would think that she got their portrait just right.

Douglas had a beautiful voice and played the guitar really well. He would sit on the quay wall and sing the latest pop songs. He could also perform hits by Edith Piaf, e.g. Allez-venez-Milord. He would also sing English shanties:

> My bonny is over the ocean.
> She drank gin. He drank rum.
> I'll tell you they had lots of fun.

His cap also never stayed empty.
Houston was so linguistically talented, he would tell the newest jokes in Italian, French, English, and even German, depending on who had gathered around him. The laughter surrounding him was always the loudest. I don't know how he managed to get tipped. I think he pretended to be a political refugee but presented it in such a funny way that no one believed him.

Casual vacation

My four London friends had set up their tent somewhere in the garden of a currently uninhabited holiday villa of a millionaire. They spent the whole day on the beach. Whenever they got hungry they counted their francs and decided whether they had enough to buy a bottle of vin du postillon, a baguette, tomatoes, grapes, and maybe even some ham. If not, they would take up their "activities" at the Promenade des Anglais.

It never took the four artists more than 20 minutes to get enough money for a meal. Well, to be honest, they were highly talented. I so would have loved to travel around the world with them as a globetrotter. My participation in their life style was hindered by me not being able to keep up with them. I got good grades in school, but that was pretty much it.

Origin

Soon, I also got a look into their families. They all came from influential families; Cynthia's family was actually aristocratic. Her mother was a court lady of the English royal family. By way of the Mitfords, she was related to Churchill's wife Clementine Hozier, another aristocratic lady.

Douglas was related to the great statesman Hamilton, who owned a large estate with its own airfield at Dungavel Castle in Scotland. Incidentally, this is where Rudolf Heß would land in 1941.

Charles was related to Lord Halifax, the English foreign minister, who was invited to the gaudy Carinhall for a hunt and was given the name Halalifax by Goering.

Houston was actually related to the prominent Chamberlain family who has brought us many great politicians and with Neville Chamberlain even gave us a prime minister. No wonder that those four vagabonds were really exceptional people and not just regular Joes.

Artists in their twilight years

Houston was still keeping a close relationship with his friends, who, like him, were living in London. Cynthia and Charles had recently made the news by creating a street picture on Trafalgar Square. They even got sued for it. Apart from that, they had a steady source of income by illustrating books.

Douglas was less successful financially with his concert for oboes and twelve type writers. He was still making music on the streets or performing as a solo entertainer in cafes and pubs.

Houston considered himself a writer without ever having had something published. He was planning a huge piece: a thousand years of world history in a thousand short stories. To summarize, the four were doing moderately well for themselves, but without the support and heritage of their rich families, they would have never been able to keep up their lifestyle into old age. They would have had to work, like I had to.

The fact that our paths have crossed, once upon a time in Nice and then again today when I met Houston at Speaker's Corner, was a coincidence. The fact that these chance meetings have blossomed into a lasting acquaintace and collaboration was destiny.

London's Pubs (1.4)

The Swan

It was time to grab a beer. A pleasant pub, rich in tradition, was situated right on the other side of the street: "The Swan." It's one of Houston's favorite hangouts, so that's where we went. The front yard was filled with wooden benches and tables but nobody was sitting there since it was too cold to sit outside. The inside of the pub however was jam-packed. We found an empty table on the right side of the entrance. A big table was filled with work colleagues taking their lunch break together. They were up to all kinds of shenanigans. As soon as a neighbor wasn't looking, his full glass was switched with an empty one. When someone left their seat for a short moment, the others would tie the sleeves of the jacket hanging over his chair, which made it hard for him to put the jacket back on later. I thought what a fun work day this was for the British. The inside of the pub was angled and convoluted. It had been remodeled and added to continually and had several balconies. A table filled with women could be reached halfway up a flight of stairs. Ten to twelve women were sitting there and playing games. They gave a very emancipated impression and obviously didn't have to stay home and cook for their husbands.

How to get a beer

I grew kind of irritated with the waiter, who passed us by several times without noticing that we had no beer. Then my new friend enlightened me and told me that in pubs, you have to get your own beer. That is why I then went to the counter, where eight taps got different kinds of beer straight out of barrels. Houston told me: "Get me a beer as well, from the fourth tap." The beer had to be paid for right away, no notches on coasters in London. Actually, not a bad system. Makes paying the check easier.

Fish and Chips

Drinking made us hungry, so Houston suggested we eat some fish and chips. They also had to be ordered at the counter and paid right away. I had meant to treat Houston to the meal anyway, but it bothered me a little that he just had me pay for his food like that. Still, the fish was very, very good – a fresh cod filet. The chips were like fries but wider and even more delicious since the crispy to soft ratio was even better balanced. My order was assigned a number that was put on a tiny banner and given to me to be put on the table. Soon, the waiter was waving a tray with a little banner with the same number on it. Everything went really smoothly. Again I thought how practical the English were. Dine-and-dash? Not even possible.

Fouquet's

The thing that happened to me at Fouquet's in Paris would have never happened to me in London. An apparently honorable, serious-looking older gentleman had addressed me in front of the restaurant. Back then, I was a "poor student" and he asked me if he could treat me to a meal. I was surprised but really grateful and we both ate well and plenty in the noble restaurant. That is, until my gracious benefactor had to go to the bathroom real quick and never returned, leaving me no choice but to pay the whole bill.

Gallows

Before Houston and I left the Swan, Houston asked me: „Did you know that four hundred years ago, the people with death sentences would get their last meal in this pub before going to the gallows?" The gallows were on the other side of the street, right where Speaker's Corner is today.

Strange how a place can just change its role like that. The place where people used to gather to amuse themselves by watching the legs of hanged men twitch involuntarily is now the place they go to laugh about the confused speeches and willing displays of the mostly psychopathic performers. It's weird, but the Genius loci somehow stayed kind of the same after all.

Since Houston is so knowledgable about English history and knows his birth city so well, I asked him to show me all of the old traditional pubs. A full program. We both had the time, my work days were over, my kids had left home, and Houston had stayed a bachelor his whole life.

The 2nd day

The house in East End (2.1)

Paddington Station

For the next day, we had planned for me to visit him at his house in East End. When I left the house the next morning, of course I had neglected to allow for rush hour. I wanted to depart from Paddington Station. However, the station was already so packed with people that getting into the train was obvious as a lost cause right away. I therefore sat down in the back on one of the benches and watched the hustle and bustle.

Every two minutes, a train arrived. People in the back were pushing the people in the front until the cars were so full that not a single person more could fit no matter how hard they tried. As soon as the next train arrived, the whole show would start anew. Really fascinating. Well, for me anyway! But the poor people who had to go through this every day...

Finally, I underwent the same procedure. In spite of the many people standing in the cars and blocking my view, I could still see pictures on the walls of shelters and helpful women passing out coffee and cake to the people seeking refuge there. Reminders of the first German air strikes on London. Again I was hit by the ever present historical awareness here. In no other city have I seen reminders of air strikes even though they had suffered from them a great deal more.

At last I reached East End and soon found Houston's house with help of his description of it. Today, East End is a chique artists' quarter, but not so long ago, it was the poorest part of London. Houston's house was built during a time when it was mainly poor dockworkers living there.

Archives, notes, and manuscripts

Houston was still busy with bringing a little order to his chaotic library. Typical for when someone is coming to "visit." "I have always had some trouble with keeping order" was how he commented on his cleaning efforts. That is probably the reason why so far, all my efforts to put my assorted stories into some kind of orderly format have failed. It takes an enormous amount of diligence. One of your great poets once said "Being a genius takes 5% talent and 90% diligence." I may have the 5% talent, but am obviously lacking the 90% diligence.

Greeting

First, we wanted to celebrate our renewed acquaintance with a glass of wine. In his wine cellar, Houston had the Port and Sherry that the British love so much, but also dry white wines from California, Chile, and Australia. He had travelled the world and therefore knew his way around a wine cellar, too. I was feeling right at home and it was obvious that he also cherished the chance to discuss his authorical problems with somebody.

The year of destiny: 1932

I will start my story collection with 1932, the year of destiny, and let the plot unravel front and back. For what reasons had he chosen this year as a crossroad, I wanted to know. For me, the date held no special symbolic power. He sees it as a pivot point in American politics. In 1932, the American establishment managed to prevent the best president the US ever had from being re-elected:

Herbert Hoover. Instead, they put one of their own into this powerful position: Franklin Delano Roosevelt. This man had also promised the American public peace, but only to snatch peace-loving voters away from his opponent. His true objective: "I need a big war." He was thinking about a war in the Pacific, a war that Hoover had wanted to prevent at all costs, and also about a war against Germany, which he wanted to utterly destroy this time.

He felt that we needed no war of conquest, no plundering hordes. The United States are so rich. If we develop our own country, build roads and railroads, bring our rich mining camps as well as our industry up to speed, then we have an actual chance of eliminating poverty. Modern technology will allow for every American to own their own house and be their own master. This vision didn't sit well with the establishment since poor and miserable people are way easier to oppress than confident, independent, and wealthy citizens.

Election result 37 %

1932, the same year that F.D. Roosevelt rose to power, presented the NSDAP's leader (Hitler) with his first big election victory, 37 % of all votes (the NSDAP was the National Socialist German Workers' Party, aka Nazi Party). Despite massive resistance from all other parties, he was finally assigned to build a government led by his party and appointed Reich Chancellor.

Thus, starting in 1932, Hitler and Roosevelt became the two most important opponents and stayed that way until the end of World War II. Roosevelt was re-elected a second time in 1936 and a third time in 1940, even though only two terms of office are allowed for in the American voting system. In 1944, he was even re-elected a fourth time, a unique occurrence in US history. However, he was already in bad health by this point, so bad that he didn't live to see the end of the war. He neither saw Hitler's end nor did he see the war in Japan end.

The dictator

In 1933, Hitler used the Enabling Act to abolish suffrage and became a dictator for life, starting in 1933 and ending with his suicide in the spring of 1945 when the Russian army invaded Berlin. It's astonishing how Hitler came to be so powerful even though only 37 % had voted for him – meaning that about 2/3 of the voters were against him. Almost as astonishing as the fact that out of 70 planned attempts on his life, not one was successful.

Munich (2.2)

The son: Randolph

Houston continued his tale. One of the first people to recognize Hitler as the political heavyweight he would become as soon as he entered the stage was an old and cunning fox: Churchill. At first, he approved of Hitler: "If my country were defeated, as Germany is, lying in ruins after the Treaty of Versailles, then I would wish for a man like him."

Hitler's political career was so interesting to Churchill right from the start that he sent his son Randolph to visit every one of Hitler's election meetings and to report back to him in London. How did he already know that this was important? Remember, this was at a time when responsible German politicians were still far from taking this newcomer seriously, in fact, they were often poking fun at him.

Randolph's father had given him orders as CEO of the Secret Service, therefore, his mission was never officially mentioned.

That is why Churchill's son lived in Munich as a private guest of the Hanfstaengl family.

Hanfstaengl

Mr. Hanfstaengl was perfectly fluent in English. Before WWI, he had owned New York's most influential gallery and had been living there for many years. When the US declared war against the German emperor in 1916, he and his family were detained and he was completely disowned. All of his earthly possessions were seized as "values of enemy people," meaning that it all happened simply because he was from Germany. And he never got any of it back. By the way, this is how all Germans were treated in the USA, in Canada, and in Australia. The same happened to farmers in German colonies in Africa.

This gross injustice had made Hanfstaengl a bitter man and it was one of the main reasons why he became one of Hitler's most fervent supporters. Since he was fluent in English, he maintained Hitler's contacts abroad, his contacts to English speaking people.

Hotel Continental

Right after Hitler's election victory of 37 %, Churchill wanted to meet him. This meeting was very easy to arrange unofficially by Churchill's own son and Hanfstaengl, and was supposed to look like a chance meeting.

At that time, Churchill was writing his historic book about his ancestor, John Churchill, Duke of Marlborough. He made it seem like he had to do research about his ancestor's famous battle of Höchstädt, during which the latter had, with the help of Prince Eugene Louis XIV, so utterly defeated the Sun King that his reign in Europe was over from that moment on.

Supposedly to this end, he was staying in Munich at the time. He had even brought along his wife, Clementine, on this ostensibly very private visit. After each political event, Hitler would frequent the Continental in the evenings. After the whole Churchill family, the son, of course, included, had had dinner, Hitler was supposed to randomly take a peek inside the dining hall and, to his great surprise, spot Churchill. The press had not been informed of Churchill's stay in Munich.

German-British collaboration?

People still speculate about just what it was that Churchill "had up his sleeve." The German-British collaboration that Hitler suggests in his book "Mein Kampf" had some support in England, even the English king at the time, King Edward VIII, was campaigning for it. Germany was supposed to clean up the continent, meaning it should fight marxist-communist Bolshevism, while the British Empire would guarantee maritime freedom.

Maybe Churchill wanted to get a feel for Hitler and how he could be used to fight Stalin's Bolshevism.

A missed chance

The Churchill family dinner was over, dessert had been eaten, and still Hitler hadn't glanced in as had been agreed upon. Hanfstaengl, who was supposed to serve as a translator, was suspecting that something had gone wrong and was on his way to make a call at the reception desk when he chanced upon Hitler in the entrance hall. "For heaven's sake! What are you waiting for? Churchill is growing impatient." But Hitler had never planned to meet his appointment. "Then at least don't show yourself as publicly here." Hitler would not even agree to this simple request. He wanted to break the deal he had himself agreed upon earlier and he wanted to do it blatantly.

A question

Why the need to insult Churchill like that? Was it just a way of showing his extreme dislike? To Hitler, Churchill had always been nothing but a "drunk journalist." As is known, Churchill had struggled with alcoholism all of his life.

Or was Hitler afraid they would find out that his entire election campaign had been financed by Baron Rothschild? It was well known that Hanfstaengl was collecting money and donations to Hitler's party from all over the English-speaking world. Rumor was that Churchill's son gave the money to Hanfstaengl in cash so that there would be no record of it.

When Hitler took over his party (he had not founded it), the party funds consisted of only 6 Mark and 12 pennies. The number of members was minimal. Hitler was supposedly assigned membership number 555 (the number of devils.) However, in 1932, the party already had its pompous headquarters in Munich. How were they able to afford that? Is it possible that the Jewish Baron Rothschild financed anti-semitism embodied by Hitler? Hitler's supporters would have never forgiven their Führer if they had found out.

Anti-semitism

„But – how absurd! Rothschild, a Jew, financing anti-semitism?" was my objection to this. "It seems absurd, yes," Houston answered. "But consider that Rothschild was an orthodox Jew and no atheist, as many modern Jews are. He was very critical of the assimilation of Germans and Jews, thinking that this would eventually annihilate the Jewish identity. If you think about that, then a certain amount of anti-semitism must have seemed quite desirable to him.

Jews and Germans

The relationship between Jews and Germans in Germany was unique back then. Nowhere else were there so many "mixed marriages." No place else saw so many Jews gain recognition as writers, virtuosos of piano or violin, or as actors. There was an incredibly rich Jewish upper class. Even renowned writers such as Thomas Mann saw no problem in marrying rich Katja Pringstein, the daughter of a Jewish banker.

Immigration restrictions

A side effect of an open discrimination of Jews that Rothschild certainly wished for was the forced emigration of many Jews. He wanted them to go to Palestine.

However, most of them wanted to go to America. That is why Rothschild made a deal with Franklin Roosevelt, cutting the contingency of Jews allowed to immigrate in half. Instead of 60,000 per year, the US now only allowed for 30,000 per year.

Tragedies ensued. For instance, Anne Frank's family was denied permission to enter the US, despite Anne's mother being a close relative of Eleanor Roosevelt, the First Lady."

To kill Hitler

How did Churchill react to this insult? "He got so mad that he proclaimed that the only goal of any political decision henceforth would be to kill Hitler. 'To kill Hitler, that was the only thing I was interested in and that made everything very easy.' He had one chance to see me in person. He will never get another – and as we know, that was true."

When he became Reich chancellor, Hitler invited Churchill to his mountain estate in Berchtesgarden 2 or 3 times. Churchill didn't even condescend to answer. Churchill, being the egomaniac he was, was never able or willing to forget that insult. The sworn enemies of the 20th century never once met in person.

Psychic

This extreme turn from sympathetic appraisal to completely negating someone's existence is hard to explain. The fact that already in 1932, Churchill felt that saving humanity and destroying Hitler were so closely linked is astonishing. Since Hitler had held no political office up to then, he hadn't even yet had a chance to commit the atrocities he later became infamous for.

Mystic powers must have had a hand in it. This fits nicely with a story that esoterics will surely enjoy. During WWI, in fire trenches in Flanders, those two sworn enemies were to be found on opposing sides at the same time and in the exact same section.

Churchill had to resign after the disaster at Gallipolli. To get back in everybody's good book, he volunteered as a soldier and fought on the frontlines. Naturally, he could have chosen to stay in the officers' mess, far away from the frontline. However, alcohol was prohibited there and that is why he preferred to live the simple life of a private in the trenches – a place where drinking your feelings was always appreciated.

Even though Churchill fancied himself a materialist to the core, he still let Crowley introduce him to black magic. Crowley claimed to have taught him his famous victory gesture as a magical symbol to ward off the extended hand of the Hitler salute. He said it actually does not symbolize victory but stands for two-horned Baphomet.

Churchill supposedly had some kind of vision when he was in the trenches. The vision revealed to him that his historic archnemesis was sitting in the enemies' trenches on the other side, but at the moment was still a little calf that had yet to grow into a mighty bull before Churchill was supposed to fight him.

Hitler recounts that he had been sitting in one part of the trenches with 10 of his fellow soldiers when suddenly, a power greater than his own free will had forced him to go to another part of the trenches. He had barely reached it when a grenade detonated right where he had been and when he came back, every single one of his comrades was dead. To Hitler, this was proof that his fight was in no way individual, but that he had been chosen and that it was his destiny to survive this battle.

The Thames terraces (2.3)

Londinium

For lunch, we wanted to go to the Thames terraces. They have wonderful restaurants there that offer excellent local and international cuisine. Also, the historic place from which London blossomed can be found there, the place the Romans already chose to start colonisation. Remnants of ancient walls can still be visited there today.

A thousand years later, normanic conquerors built a fortress and a royal palace, the Tower. To this day, the Tower still fascinates people with its simple elegance. It is a place for meditation. What's more, we could reach it by foot. On our way there, Houston told me even more stories, they just came bursting out of him. Give him a cue and he will tell you a whole story about it.

Satirical song

Do you know how the French got back at Marlborough after they were defeated in Höchstädt? They made him the butt of a joke by writing a satirical song about him that every child knows by the time it goes to kindergarten.

Marlborough s'en va-t-en guerre
Il a mis ses culottes à l'envers

He goes to war, but his pants are on backwards. This big hero can't even put on his own pants right.

Are you sure about that, dear friend? As far as I know, it was „le bon roi Dagobert qui a mis ses culottes à l´envers?"

Prince Eugene

The thing that probably hurt the Sun King most was that it had to be Prince Eugene of all people, leading the Austrian troops, who defeated him side by side with the English military. Initially, Prince Eugene had wanted to start his military career under Louis XIV. The latter had, however, only laughed at him, saying: "My royal army does certainly not need a weakling like you."

After this, the young prince introduced himself to the Hapsburg emperor in Vienna and became a great general. He defeated not only the Turks, but also, who'd have guessed, imperial France itself.

Incidentally, the prince came from a dynasty related to all leading families in Europe. That is why, proud of his heritage, he always signed in three languages. His first name, Eugenio, in Italian, his royal title, von, in German, and Savoy in French. You might call him the epitome of a true European.

Höchstädt

Naturally, big victories such as this one have to be documented accordingly. That is why historiographs accompanied all armies during their battles. The posthumous fame of these battles was supposed to last centuries and could only be guaranteed by having written records of it. These civil servants were amongst the most well-paid employees of both the English and the French king. Their annual income matched up to that of a general.

However, their skills were really put to a test during the battle of Höchstädt. They weren't able to properly reproduce the two umlaut vowels ö and ä in English. Furthermore, the ch gave them a headache since it is a sound that doesn't exist in the English phoneme inventory. And then there was this terrible scht sound right in the middle of the word! The poor English historiographs were at their wits' end when confronted with this pesky unpronounceable name. They were desperate. And so, they asked if there was some other town close by that might be easier to pronounce in English. There was indeed: the village Blindheim or, in a Swabian dialect, Blendheim (Höchstädt lies on the Danube, close to Ulm). They used Blendheim and in their accounts of the battle, it became Blenheim because they hadn't heard the d in its name.

As far as they were concerned, they had solved their linguistic problem in an acceptable manner. That is how to the English, this battle became known as the Battle of Blenheim. And the same name was given to the palace the grateful English king gave to his victorious general as a present.

Blenheim Palace

To this day, this magnificent palace is bequeathed to the first-born descendant of the Duke of Marlborough. Churchill was very proud of the fact that he had been born in this palace, even though his father was only third in line and the palace didn't belong to him. Still, Churchill took it as a sign that he was born there anyway, in some way making him Marlborough's actual successor.

The great ball

The oldest brother hosted a great ball each year and invited all of his relatives to join him. Churchill's mother, a vivacious and strikingly beautiful young woman, had married his father, Randolphe Churchill, six months prior to the ball and obviously didn't want to miss an event like that. She was dancing passionately, as always, when suddenly she had violent contractions and only just managed to reach the toilet in time.

She had just sat down when young Winston, in a case of precipitate labor, shot out of her body. Luckily, she was able to grab his feet just before he fell into the septic tank.

At this point in the story, I interrupted Houston and said: "Be honest, now you are letting your imagination run wild." "I'm sure a palace like that would have already had water closets by then." "Well, that may be, but the fact is that Churchill was born in a royal palace but in a place that was quite un-royal."

His birth also raises the question if he was born prematurely when he was only six months old. This was widely assumed at first since no more months had passed between the wedding and his birth. By now, the official consensus is that when she got married, Jenny was already three months pregnant. And the toilet has officially become a dressing room or a vestibule.

Syphilis

The second question that arose was whether Randolph was Churchill's biological father. In fact, as is widely known, he had a disease that made him a rather undesirable partner for young girls. Because of this same disease, Randolph died early on, but not before Churchill's mother fell pregnant a second time. This time, it was made official that he was not the father of this second child.

And so Churchill got a half-brother and rumors started, stating that Winston Churchill's biological father also wasn't his mother's husband. It is unclear if Churchill himself knew about this. After all, as soon as he came of age, he was sent to live in the USA with Cockran, who made Winston's schooling and political education his objective.

Cockran was one of the most influential US politicians of his time. He was a presidential candidate four times and each time, he only lost by a narrow margin. In addition, he was a moderately well-known writer. Churchill saw both him and Disraeli, a great English politician and important writer, as his big idols.

And in fact, Churchill can be compared to both of them. Next to his political posts, he has also accomplished a great deal as both a journalist and an author of books. It isn't for nothing that he received the Nobel Prize for Literature.

Baptismal song

Houston confessed that he had once entertained the idea of writing a musical with Douglas. In this musical, he had wanted to display this situation, amongst others, in a satirical manner.

In order to spare Cockran the trouble that came with an illegitimate child, something that could not have been circumvented in the USA, Baron von Rothschild asked his closest associate, Randolph Churchill, to get his friend out of this predicament and marry Jenny.

The musical was supposed to summarize all that in a quatrain.
> First Cockran could put his cock in
> Then it's the mister Baron's win
> Just her dear husband had no luck
With his poor syphilitic cock
Douglas composed a canon for three voices with those lyrics. He called it Baptismal Song and as a melody used the River Kwai March, a melody to which English soldiers were singing: Hitler has only got one ball.

For example, Randolph had convinced Queen Victoria to give Baron von Rothschild his title, even though Victoria felt it would be impossible to grant a Jew any noble title. Randolph supposedly answered: "Your majesty, if you didn't have his money, you would not be able to rule your empire."

Even back then, Baron von Rothschild was the richest man on earth. What's more, he allegedly felt great affection for Jenny. Fake news even writes that he was Churchill's father.

Fake news also report him to be Adolf Hitler's father, which would make those bitter enemies half-brothers. In fact, the two do share similar political views. Their take on social darwinism and their conviction that the law of might is always right are exactly the same.

Tower (2.4)

William the Conqueror

By then, we had walked along the river and gotten close to the Tower. This was also one of Houston's favorite places in London. From the Thames terraces, you have a wonderful view of the fortress with its four slender corner towers and the Tower Bridge, as well as on the Thames that runs its broad course right behind it. This building is a museum today and contains a thousand years of living history. Its story goes from its builder, William the Conqueror, who used it as a fortress and a royal palace, to medieval times when it was used as a prison.

Henry the VIII

This is where Henry the VIII had his second wife, Anne Boleyn, executed. She is the mother of Elizabeth the Great. She is also the reason Henry parted ways with Rome after a lengthy correspondence with Luther as the Pope would not grant him the right to divorce his first wife. Outraged, Henry founded the Anglican Church, making himself its high priest, a position currently occupied by Queen Elizabeth II. Now he no longer needed the Pope's permission.
His fifth wife, Katherine Howard, was also executed here.

Lady Jane Grey

An especially tragic story is that of the decapitation of the young Nine Days' Queen, Lady Jane Grey. Her story has touched all of Europe. The great German writer Fontane even composed a ballad about her and many poets have written about her execution in the Tower.

The Tower's last prisoner was Rudolf Heß in 1941.

The Yeomen Warders still wear their dapper uniform, black with red edgings, every day, not only when there's a festival – just like they did back then. A good type of gin was named after their popular nickname: beefeater.

Lamb or mutton

As an aperitif, we indulged in that very same gin. Not usual, but still. I have forgotten the name of the restaurant: Cutty Sark, Coppa Club, or Byward Kitchen. Anyway, its location was unique. The food was exquisite and typically English. English cuisine has a bad reputation, but they sure know how to prepare lamb like nobody else does. Our lamb chops with grilled cherry tomatoes were excellent.

Even our food gave Houston cause to tell stories. Our people's history lives on through language as well. When the Normans came to England as its new conquerors, they brought with them their Old French dialect. Despite being of Germanic descent, they, as a minority group in Normandy, had adopted the dialect spoken there. For centuries, the ruling class spoke this Old French dialect while the servants naturally continued to use their ancestral Anglo-saxon.

35

That is why the animals were called sheep and lambs for as long as they were out on the fields, but as soon as they were served as a meal to the rulers, they were called mutton (French: mouton). Calves became veal (French: veau), oxen became beef (French: boeuf). The Germanic word tisch became table and the word tisch or, in English, dish, now assumed its modern meaning of meal, food.

Richard the Lionheart

The great English national hero of the crusades, Richard Coeur de lion or Lionheart, still spoke this Old French dialect. Back then, Normandy still belonged to England, as did Aquitaine. It was only when England developed a sense of national identity that those French estates in continental France were lost. But to get there, it took the Hundred Years' War.

It was national saint Jeanne d'Arc, the Maid of Orleans, who ushered in the final phase of this prolonged war. Tradition and history are all present in this one place. And in France and England, even little children already know their national heroes and their history and are proud of it. Meanwhile, young people in Germany only learn that there were concentration camps in Dachau and Auschwitz.

A reunion after so many years (2.5)

Cynthia

I was really looking forward to the evening. We would meet in Houston's house and my old friends from Nice had promised to come. I was curious to see what they looked like after all these years. Would I still recognize them? Would they still recognize me?

Cynthia was the first to come through the door. She was as beautiful as ever. She greeted me with a kiss on the lips. Ah, so she also hadn't forgotten that it had been her who had made a real man out of me, back then, on the beach in Nice.

Then came her partner, Charles. He had been a radiant guy, always smiling ear to ear. He was still a very handsome man with a stately frame. Douglas, our musician, was a bit late. I wondered how the ideals of our youth had held up: be absolutely free, don't make commitments, don't accept responsibility. While they were young, this worked out okay, but it became harder and harder over the years.

Having a job is the backbone of life, also financially speaking. Well, none of them had wanted regulated working hours and a steady income, but that was only possible because they all came from very wealthy families and could live off their inheritance.

Edward VIII

Cynthia's mother worked at the royal court of King Edward VIII. The king, like Cynthia's family, was very pro-German, unlike the general atmosphere in England. All of my friends on that evening were also Germanophiles, otherwise they certainly wouldn't have let me, a German, into their inner circle. Our conversations that evening centered on German-English relations.

Cynthia began to talk. She said that Edward VIII was a decidedly big fan of Hitler. He visited him several times in Germany. The Marxist-Leninist groups, who also wanted to abolish monarchy in England, were a cause of great concern to him. Hitler had rid Germany of this 'rabble.' His vision of the future saw Germany bring order to the continent by fighting Stalin's Bolshevism while England, the big empire, would guarantee free seafare on every ocean.

As Edward believed, only the white race would be able to bring order to a world that was on the brink of breaking apart due to struggles for independency in the colonies.

Only recently, a video has surfaced that shows Edward VIII teaching his five-year-old niece Elisabeth how to do the Hitler salute. At the moment, the press has no campaign against the royal family on its agenda, so the video wasn't turned into a big scandal.

Wallis Simpson shot this video. Two years later, Edward VIII took a picture of the royal family. On it, you can see that even the Queen Mum raises her hand to the Hitler salute, alongside Elisabeth. The man who would go on to become George VI later on is bending down to little Margret.

However, the king's refusal to wage war against Germany as long as he was king lead to pro-war parties, most of all Churchill, to try to find a way to have him overthrown.

Wallis Simpson

The leverage they had to overthrow the king, or rather to make him resign, was Mrs. Wallis Simpson. She was an American actress who, after her divorce, had married the super-rich businessman Simpson. Edward VIII took a liking to her and so she became his mistress. Her husband travelled around all year on business, visiting the world's capitals and the several mistresses he himself had there.

He even felt flattered by the fact that the king of the biggest world empire, the Emperor of India, liked his wife and his wife was thankful that he stayed her husband and thus financed her lavish lifestyle. She couldn't live off the precious jewels the king showered her with and that is why she never even considered a divorce. Marriage was her safety net.

Also, she was lacking nothing, the king openly took her to parties, even to Buckingham Palace.

Queen Mary

Only the Queen Mum, a very elegant queen, prudent and respectful of etiquette, always insisted that everyone act according to their social standing.

When she was present, Wallis Simpson was not allowed to show up. Firstly, she was not royalty, secondly, she wasn't even English and what's more, she was married and, how appalling, her first marriage had ended in divorce.

Edward VIII knew that he could never make her his queen; as the high priest of the Anglican Church, it was out of the question for him to have a divorcee by his side. Especially not if the divorced husband was still alive.

However, Edward VIII wasn't planning on marrying her. Why would he? They were leading a happy, content life together and were in want of nothing.

Opponents

A king was supposed to marry and sire an heir to the throne. This was not possible with Wallis Simpson. The pro-war party, wanting to get rid of a king who ruled out any chance of waging a war on Germany, tried blackmailing him: if he didn't abdicate voluntarily, a press campaign against Wallis Simpson would be started. This campaign would compromise the royal family so much that the monarchy itself would stand no chance.

Edward VIII was reminded of the fate of the Russian Tsar and his family in Saint Petersburg. When the overthrown Tsar had asked his English cousin to grant him and his family refuge in England, Edward wasn't able to do so. The according promise his father, George V, had already given was thwarted by others. He was not allowed to take his cousin and his family in, even though the Tsar and Russia were an English ally in their fight against the German emperor.

In addition, George V was forced to change his German-sounding name, Sachsen-Coburg Gotha, into Windsor.

Press scandal

To give Edward VIII a first taste of what kind of press scandals he could expect, a scandalous story was printed, showing Wallis Simpson nude and dancing on tables in Buckingham Palace in front of full halls.

It was reported that Simpson had worked in Shanghai brothels where she had learned devious sexual practices, which explained why the king had fallen for her.

None of that was true. And even though the newspapers later had to concede that it had all been fictitious, it still had an incredible impact. The English did not want a king of that sort nor a woman of that sort to lead them.

Assassination attempt

"You don't get rid of a king with court orders – you need to assassinate him." That was what Churchill thought when, on July 16, 1936, he decided to get rid of King Edward VIII. Despite the scandalous stories that especially Churchill's friend Hearst, America's biggest newspaper tycoon, helped perpetuate, Edward still wasn't willing to abdicate.

The military secret service MI5 used the "Double bound" tactic, meaning they turned an assassin they themselves had trained so that the public thought he was sent by the enemy. That is what happened with Jerome Branningham, who was smuggled into the Irish IRA shortly before the assassination attempt. The attempt failed because local police, who weren't in on the ploy, protected the king's life. Still, the king got so scared by the attempt on his life that he finally signed the document of abdication.

Abdication

The king was helpless. He stood no chance, neither against the press nor the secret service. That is why finally, he abdicated, making his brother George VI heir apparent. However, George VI had to meet the conditio sine qua non – he had to support the war against Germany. The new king also didn't think this war was in England's best interests. It was mainly American economic managers and Wallstreet's high finance who wanted to eliminate the German competition.

Another reason why he only reluctantly accepted the crown was that he stuttered. He could not think of anything worse than having to hold a public speech. But despite all this, he had to accept his new responsibility.

The King's Speech

With help of a language instructor, and by putting in extreme effort, he managed to record a flawless speech. This historic address, "The King's Speech," can be downloaded from the Internet at any time. There is even a movie about it. The speech was recorded several weeks before the war began and could therefore be broadcast immediately after the first shootout in Gdansk.

The document of abdication had to be signed by all brothers, meaning Edward VIII; the new king, George VI; and the youngest brother, the first Duke of Kent. Edward VIII and his wife had to go into exile. The new king could only grant his brother the right to put foot on English soil in case of familial incidents, like, for example, the death of their mother.

Tall stories

A lie made it around the world, a lie about the big love story of the century: a king abdicates so he's able to marry the woman he loves. Unto this day, this version is repeated as true. The truth is, however, that no king of any country in this world has ever had to abdicate because of a mistress and we know that in this case, it was also not the actual reason for Edward's abdication.

Still, the inconsistencies of the official version only become obvious once you have heard Cynthia's alternative story. Since we rarely get to experience historic events ourselves, we depend on the press to tell us what happened. If all newspapers report the same facts because they all belong to one and the same publisher, we, the readers, will accept even the most blatant lies. The manipulative power of the press is absolute, and our disinformation is, too.

An extraordinary family (2.6)

The Mitfords

Cynthia had another surprising story in store for us. She told us about a truly extraordinary family that she is actually even related to. It's the family of the British nobleman David Freeman-Mitford, the second Baron Redesdale. This aristocrat harbored a great dislike for British schools.

After the First World War, the UK had found schools to be a great instrument of national dulling. The USA had realized that right from the start. And since the Second World War, Germany is also chasing the same goal. By now, we have almost reached the international standard, most German students are barely able to read or write. I'm not even going to mention maths.

Anyway, the duke had his son and his six daughters home-schooled by private teachers. And that is why each of his descendants developed an independent and completely individual personality.

Jessica was completely taken with communism, something that is very rare in aristocratic families. She fought in the Spanish Civil War against Franco alongside the Communist International.

Diana was drawn to fascist ideology and went on and on about Mussolini and Hitler. She even married the British fascist leader Mosley.

Nancy became a famous writer.

The youngest daughter, Deborah, was content with becoming the Duchess of Devonshire by marriage.

Thomas also chose a rather conventional path by studying in Oxford and becoming a judge. He stayed single.

Pamela was bored by the life an American millionaire could offer her and preferred the adventures and affairs of a soldier of fortune and amateur jockey. That is why she divorced her American husband.

And lastly, Unity, probably the biggest surprise to us: she became Hitler's British mistress.

The British mistress

In late 1934, Unity travelled to Munich. It wasn't hard to find Hitler in his favorite pub there, the Osteria Bavaria.

What happened between them was, as the French call it, a coup de foudre – love at first sight. She was tall, 1.80 meters, very tall for a woman back then, and had blond hair and blue eyes. To Hitler, she was the ideal epitome of a noble Germanic woman, the perfect Aryan lady.

Her middle Name, Valkyrie, which she later changed to Walküre to make it sound more German, was a sign to Hitler, a great admirer of Wagner.

And when she told him that her grandfather, the first Baron of Redesdale, had been the one to translate the works of Houston-Stewart-Chamberlain from German to English, Hitler was irrevocably smitten.

Houston Steward Chamberlain

Even though H.S.C. was an Englishman, he still spent most of his adolescence in France. He was travelling all through Europe for many years and finally settled down in Bayreuth, Germany, where he married Richard Wagner's daughter, Eva Wagner.

His works were all written in German and he even became a German citizen by law. His manuscripts brought him great success, in Germany as well as in England, thanks to Unity's grandfather's translation. In "The Foundations of the 19th century," he explains his racist doctrine. It became the foundation for Hitler's conviction that a superior race has to put the world in order and for Hitler, that race was the Aryan race – the Germans.

Incidentally, Churchill was also fully convinced of H.S.C.'s theories, he just didn't want to let the role of this "most noble" race go to the Germans.

Jealousy

Hitler often took Unity to his mountain estate in Berchtesgarden. For the Olympic Games in Berlin, he lent her his Mercedes. He invited her to the Bayreuth Wagner Festival. And when Austria became part of the German Reich, she was standing right next to him on the Heldenplatz in Vienna.

Eva Braun didn't like this one bit. She was living on the mountain estate under the guise of being an employee of Hitler's court photographer, Hoffmann. Hitler didn't want their relationship to become public.

She was never allowed to appear publicly with him. "I am married to Germany. My female followers would never forgive me if they knew I had a paramour."

And indeed, the German public only got wind of their relationship after the war had already ended. It also became known that Eva Braun had been forced to get sterilized because Hitler thought it would be absolutely impossible for him, the Führer, to have an illegitimate child.

Castro

I thought about a story very similar to this one. The great revolutionary Fidel Castro had a German lover who lived in America. It appears that the relationship was built on genuine feelings and even when the woman got pregnant, they were both overjoyed. However, after a while, doubts arose and Castro thought that his fellow revolutionaries might resent their leader for having private love affairs. He therefore had the poor girl kidnapped and the pregnancy terminated against her will in a clinic in Havanna.

Wedding

However, Hitler didn't have the same problems with Unity Mitford. She was in the center of attention and admiration. She even held speeches about the advantages England would have if a man like Hitler improved Germany's standing in the world.

Her sister Diana had her wedding to Mosley in Goebbels's Villa in Grunewald in Berlin. Her parents travelled there from England and were greeted by Hitler as if they were official government representatives. All this caused Eva Braun so much pain that she even attempted suicide.

A tragic ending

In August 1939, Unity and Hitler were visiting the Bayreuth festival. That is where he told her that England was dead set on declaring war on Germany and that he saw no way of preventing it. He assured her that both she and her sister Diana were free to leave Germany.

Diana left, Unity stayed. She just couldn't believe it. She loved both countries. Her dream was: the German army and the English navy could rule the world. And now, just like in WWI, those two countries were going to tear each other apart.

Suicide

On September 1, 1939, the first shot was fired in Gdansk. On September 3, when England declared war on Germany, Unity shot herself in the head with an automatic pistol on Königinnenstraße in Munich.

She was severly injured when she was brought to a clinic. She had left a suicide note for Hitler and had put the golden party badge engraved with her name that Hitler had had made for her personally right next to it. She wrote that she couldn't survive the fact that the two countries she loved so much were now fighting a war against each other.

This note hasn't survived the war, it doesn't exist anymore, which is why objectors claim it has never existed.

Hitler visited Unity in the clinic. She was paralyzed on one side and couldn't talk anymore. He had brought her golden badge back to her. She took it, put it in her mouth and swallowed it. Hitler said to his photographer Hoffmann, who had come along: "I am starting to become afraid."

Grass

This scene must be what Günther Grass thought of when little Oscar, a character in his book *The Tin Drum*, opens the needle of the party badge that his step-father later swallows, which leads to his death.

Partial recovery and early death

German doctors refused to surgically remove the bullet from Unity's brain. If anything had gone wrong during that operation, the world press would have called it an intentional killing on Hitler's behalf. That is why she was brought to Switzerland, but the Swiss doctors also didn't want to do the risky operation. Hitler paid for all of this himself.

As soon as her condition was stable enough, her parents had her transferred to England. But even there, doctors were refusing to operate on her. The procedure was just too risky.

Inch Kenneth

So, she went on to live with her mother on a secluded Scottish Hebridean island that belonged to her father. Apparently, her recovery went so well that eventually, she was even able to once again drive a car by herself. However, meningitis caused by the bullet in her head lead to her dying when she was only 33 years old.

Diana Mitford

She returned to England where, apparently, she heavily criticized her uncle, Winston Churchill.

Clementine Hozier, Churchill's wife, was one of the Mitford daughters' aunts. Their famous grandfather who had translated H.S.C.'s works had had a love affair with love-crazed Lady Blanche, whose husband was verifiably sterile. Clementine was his daughter and that is how the families saw it as well.

"What are you trying to achieve? Why do you want this war at all costs?"

"If there had been no war then you would have soon realized why it was necessary."

„Yes, because then a freeway and a railway line would have been built through the Polish Corridor, connecting Frankfurt an der Oder to Königsberg. The Polish would have made considerable amounts of money in transit fees, year after year, without having to lift a finger and at no cost to them. They were going to agree to that until you urged them to decline by making them all kinds of absurd promises. You told them they would get all of Silesia, East Prussia, and Brandenburg, including Berlin. And what do they have now instead? Warsaw in ruins."

"That may be true, but that would have only been Hitler's first step on his way to world domination."

"But what you did was incite the end of the British world empire. While our forces are tied up fighting this war, we won't be able to control our colonies and they will win back their independence."

"Listen to you gab. I will have you arrested for not knowing when to shut your big mouth." And that is what happened. Diana was sent to an internment camp.

Mosley

Incidentally, his brother is the famous race-car driver. He also returned to England, wanting to clean out the Augean stable. However, his fascist party stood no chance in England. He admitted defeat himself: "When you're buried underneath the dirt, you have no way of cleaning it up."

Trump

In 2017, a crass outsider wanted to dry up the swamp Washington had become. It seems that by now, he himself has gotten stuck in it. He was elected because people believed he could prevent the planned war on Russia. Today, he isn't even allowed to talk to Putin. Should proof surface that he or one of his associates had already contacted Putin earlier, an impeachment will be initiated.

Trials are arduous. Maybe the CIA can think of a quicker way to get rid of him.

Preparing for war (2.7)

Gandhi's letter

Charles contributed the following story. Friends of Gandhi who appreciated his desire for peace urged him to prevent the impending world war. He actually wrote Hitler a letter that starts like this:

Dear friend,

I know that you are not the monster your enemies make you out to be, but you are the only one who can still prevent this war. Bear in mind how much I have achieved with non-violent resistance. Do not give Roosevelt and Churchill the chance to start a big war.

This is not the exact wording of the letter but only its content. The letter never reached Hitler, it was intercepted. After all, England was still the ruling colonial power in India.

However, Gandhi did successfully refuse to send Indian soldiers into the war. In WWI, millions of Indians had been fighting. But the struggle over preventing a connection between Frankfurt an der Oder and Königsberg? "Our citizens don't have to risk their lives for that."

In all probability, the letter would not have changed Hitler's course of action anyway. He knew that since 1932, Roosevelt had been dead set on fighting this war, a war that had to happen under all circumstances and under no matter what pretext.

Gandhi's 2nd letter

Two of Gandhi's phrases in particular had provoked outrage among the English. Firstly, his greeting, "Dear friend" and secondly "I know that you are not the monster your enemies make you out to be." He was forced to write Hitler a second letter before Christmas in which he had to relativize his previous statements. However, there are phrases in this second letter that can in no way have been written by Gandhi himself. There is no doubt that these phrases are fake. It is likely that this letter did reach its addressee. You can read this letter on the Internet.

Half-naked fakir

Churchill's opinion on Gandhi was clear. He was outraged by this "half-naked fakir" who was insolent enough to dare to talk to an English governor. When Gandhi went on his hunger strikes, Churchill didn't see why they couldn't just let him starve.

Inferior race

Incidentally, his opinion on the matter coincides with Hitler's. The latter had repeatedly offered England to use his military forces to overpower Indian revolutionaries, to even have Gandhi and 200 of his most influential companions killed during a fight. India was supposed to stay an English colony at all costs because the Indians themselves, as an inferior race, were not able to govern a state as far as he was concerned.

Indo-Germanic ancestry

This is actually quite astonishing since Hitler should have known that the tall, fair-skinned warriors who migrated to this subcontinent from the North were "Aryans." They dominated the small, dark-skinned natives. The word Indo-Germanic documents that. German scientists were leading forces in researching the way Indo-Germanic languages are related. Sanskrit was known best by German professors. Vedan and Upanishad literature, the brilliant achievements of an Old Indian high culture, were discovered in German universities. Even Hitler's symbol, the swastika, comes from there and the English word for it is its original name in Sanskrit. It symbolizes the sun wheel and was used as a symbol of good fortune by the immigrant Aryans back then.

Subhash Chandra Bose

And Hitler was therefore also blind to the possibilities a collaboration with Bose could have opened up. This man, who is mostly unknown in Europe, was one of the great charismatic leaders during the Indian liberation movement. Today, his statue stands in Amritsar. Thanks to the Internet, anyone can learn about him. He didn't believe that Gandhi's peaceful method would lead to India winning its independence. He was even afraid that the Indians alone would not be able to achieve independence. In his opinion, they desperately needed support from foreign military forces. He was counting on Germany and Japan to help. But, as was said before, he had no luck with Hitler. However, while running its course, the war stirred up some chaos and that is why it was only in 1942 that he, Ribbentrop, and Hitler could meet.

Volunteers

Gandhi had refused to compel Indians to join the military just so a land dispute over a few square kilometers in the Polish Corridor could be settled. Still, there were volunteers, mostly Sikhs, who signed up by the millions to fight for the British in Africa, Asia, and Europe. This phenomenon is hard to explain. Did they do it because they had to financially? Today, about 100,000 Africans are probably fighting for the Jihad only so they can make ends meet with the pay they get. Or is it that the Sikh warrior caste is just so fixated on fighting? Sadly, 3.5 million lost their lives during that fight in WWII. That makes India's death toll in World War II one of the highest, following those of Russia, Germany, Japan, and Poland.

The Indian Legion

Many Sikhs were captured by German and Japanese troops. Bose recruited volunteers among those prisoners, who were now supposed to fight against England. They swore loyalty to both him and Hitler and were called the Indian Legion. Instead of the steel helmets, they were allowed to wear their turbans on the frontlines. These turbans are part of their Hindu religion and not to be confused with the Muslim head dress.

Wife and daughter

Bose did in no way agree with Hitler on everything. Most of all, he was opposed to his Race Laws that, for example, outlawed the marriage between not only a German citizen and a Jewish person, but also an Indian citizen. He himself had a German wife, or rather, an Austrian wife. His only daughter, Anita, who was born in 1938, still lives in Augsburg to this day. She is a distinguished professor, an emeritus, and the mother of three children. So, in a way, Bose lives on in Germany through his three grandchildren. He himself died during a plane crash on August 18, 1945 in Taiwan. He had organized attacks against the Americans there.

Blood group

Charles's stories were completely new to me. But then I remembered that a close relative of mine, Dr. Schell, who back then was still a student of medicine, had written his doctor's thesis on blood groups. A comparison of the percentage distribution of blood groups between Sikhs and Germans was meant to give possible clues about an ancestral kinship of the two. I don't remember which results his thesis yielded and whether it had any far-reaching consequences. I do remember, however, that he described his collaboration with the Sikhs as friendly and cooperative.

Weaponry transports

Their experiences in WWI had taught the Americans that the submarines made it hard for them to transport arms to England across the Atlantic. German submarines sank 3,500 ships, which is why trucks, ammunition, tanks, guns, and canons were brought to England as early as 1932 so that everything would be in place when the war started. Since the elected government representatives, the Senate and Congress, weren't supposed to know about it, the transports could not become official. That is why a foreigner, the Greek shipowner Onassis, got the job because his cargo wasn't checked.

Onassis

Roosevelt and Churchill had already known him for quite a while since they were in the same Masonic Lodge. Being a Greek citizen, he didn't have to pay taxes, which made their deal a very inexpensive one for the Americans. Churchill had instated tax exemption for rich people during the First World War, the requirement being that they had to force the pro-German and ethnically German Greek king to emigrate.

With a hundred ships that belonged to him, Onassis had quite the capacity to offer. However, a few years before the war broke out, this suddenly didn't seem to be enough for Roosevelt anymore. He therefore suspended his own commanders and admirals because their activities were documented, but neither the American public nor the governement itself were yet allowed to know about those military transports. Onassis's activities on the other hand were of no interest since he was a private citizen and a foreigner to boot. This made it possible for him to transport arms to England with American battleships that weren't registered.

Legally, that wasn't quite okay. The ruse would however only become known after the war had already ended. Onassis was then sentenced to pay a fine of 7 million dollars – the US are a constitutional country, after all. This fine wasn't based on the illegal transports but on a paragraph that states that the American navy can only be commanded by an American citizen – and, after all, Onassis was Greek.

The contracting authority, Roosevelt, had already died by the time Onassis was sentenced. But, being the president, he couldn't have been prosecuted anyway.

Yacht Christina

Of course, Onassis showed his gratitude for getting these lucrative jobs. Once a year, he invited all of America's prominent politicians to join him on his luxurious yacht, Christina – at the time, the most luxurious yacht of all.

He had named the yacht after his daughter. Churchill was his guest of honor and gladly accepted the invitation long into his old age. Even when he was already confined to his wheelchair and his favorite daughter Sarah had to take care of him.

Each year, the Kennedys also took part. That is how Onassis was introduced to Jacqueline, who at the time was still married to husband John F. Kennedy but would later become Onassis's wife. Back then, she was enraptured by opera diva Callas, Onassis's wife at the time, who sang her arias exclusively for these prominent guests.

To Churchill, those select few were just like him – the overhumans Nietzsche had predicted. "Humans will decline, but humans are only a transition" is what the philosopher writes in The Antichrist. And this elite group had already reached the overhuman state, free from Christian morality.

They stood in contrast to the too big majority of others. Churchill considered the common people of his own country to belong to this second group, which is why to him, their death meant nothing.

Snappy come-back

While picturing Churchill in his wheelchair, Charles remembered another little anecdote. Even when he had already gotten very old, Churchill still had someone wheel him into the parliament. A few young parliamentarians without any respect for the superhero in his current state were talking smack: "What is this doddery old man still doing here? He can hardly talk anymore. They say he is so demented that he doesn't even know where he is." That is when the almost 90-year-old turned and said: "They also say he's deaf and dumb."

Churchill's reason for wanting to be brought into parliament even though he could no longer participate in discussions was this: as long as the parliamentarians see me there, they will be guaranteed not to decide anything that is good for Germany even in the slightest.

German reality (2.8)

For it or against it

The five of us were already quite drunk and even though our "stories" weren't always funny, there were still a lot of laughs going around. I was asked to share my perspective on how Hitler was seen from a German point of view.

Well, when the war started, I was only three and a half years old, but even so, some things were etched into my young brain.

Right from the start, my parents were against Hitler, putting us at a disadvantage several times. Naturally, I shared my parents' opinion and could not understand how good acquaintances who had always been friendly with us could be so taken with Hitler.

Even an uncle of mine was defending Hitler, which is why there were family disputes any time he was on home leave.

From today's view, my family was completely unpolitical and none of us ever read "Mein Kampf." Being for or against Hitler wasn't something that was decided with political arguments. It was a decision based on emotions, today we would say we "trusted our gut feeling."

In my experience, most of those who joined the Nazi party also didn't do it because they agreed with Hitler's party line but rather because they hoped it would bring them benefits. They were the typical opportunistic followers who pay court to successful parties everywhere.

No Jews allowed

The Gauleiter (regional leader) lived on the other side of the street from us. He critized the fact that our shop door had no "No Jews allowed" sign. "There is not a single Jew living in our neighborhood, I can save myself the money" is what my dad said. And he was right.

It was only after the war, at the age of 20, that I first met some Jews.

However, the Gauleiter thought that "that's not what it's about, it is a question of showing the proper attitude."

He had no success. He also ran into a wall with my grandfather, who had a shop in the city center and a Jewish regular customer. "That guy has been coming to my shop for over 10 years and as long as he pays me, he'll get what he wants here." That was a very brave statement and not every shop owner would have dared to give a Gauleiter that kind of answer.

Jokes

Mrs. Grimme, a typically proletarian woman with some dramatic talent, used to come to our store regularly. She would burst through the door into the shop where several customers were waiting their turn and yell dramatically at the top of her lungs "Hitler has lost his eraser!" "Bullshit!" "No, it's true, because Churchill found it! Now he's erasing our cities." Today, nobody remembers that Hitler's speech after the first bomb attack on the German civil population was: If he attacks German cities that aren't military targets, then I will erase English cities in return.

Some other time, she came in and said "Have you heard? Goebbels went to the hospital."

"What's wrong with him?"

"He had to undergo surgery."

"What kind of surgery?"

"They had to relocate his ears."

"There's no such thing."

"Oh, but there is! They had to relocate his ears to the back of his head so he could open his mouth even wider!"

Good old Mrs. Grimme risked a lot by doing that. If someone had reported her, she would have been arrested. Not only was it forbidden to make jokes about Hitler; his ministers, including his minister of propaganda Goebbels, were also taboo.

Weiß – Ferdl

A popular comedian from Munich, Weiß-Ferdl, was well-known because during his comedic routine, he would pose as a fishmonger on Viktualienmarkt, advertising the quality of his fish with the following words:

Herring, herring

Fat like Goering.

Hermann Goering was Hitler's second in command after Heß had been taken prisoner in England.

Thanks to his popularity, Weiß-Ferdl was released from jail after three days. His fishmonger skit stayed part of his routine and everybody was curious how he would advertise his fish now. And there he was, yelling like a market crier:

Herring, Herring

As fat..........as the last time

Communist underground

In secret, there still were "Reds" in Germany who, even after the attack on Russia, still sympathized with Stalin. This came up again and again in conversations. Even as a child, I heard a lot more than the adults counted on. Like, for example, a customer, Mrs. Fritz, who, after the catastrophe of Stalingrad, joyfully told my mother: "When Stalin wins, I will move into your beautiful house and you can go live in an appartement."

I totally got that Mrs. Fritz would have liked to move into our house. What I didn't understand was what Stalin had to do with that. But, of course, she would have been right if the Soviets had taken over our region like they did later on in the GDR.

Nursery rhymes

Her small daughter Rita went to kindergarten with me and she sang us a funny song that we all sang along with enthusiastically without knowing what we were singing.

> Everything passes,
> Everything will be over
> Even Hitler and his party will have to move over.

I don't know who rewrote the beautiful folk song. Its original text is a hopeful reminder that every December will be followed by May.

Sister Selma

Even in kindergarten, everything passes and the times changed. The kids were now to be educated in the spirit of National Socialism. Our plump sister Selma with her white bonnet and her blue-and-white striped nurse's dress had to give way to a strict female party member.

Sister Selma took care of 60 girls and boys of the ages of 4 to 6 without any help. She taught us how to sing, craft, crochet, and even the boys had to learn how to knit. I, however, was at a total loss there because I kept dropping the stitches.

There was one big room for all of us, but we spent most of our time in the garden. There was a big meadow with some trees and gymnastic bars. We weren't allowed to climb the trees, but did it anyway when Sister Selma wasn't looking. There was a big fuss when a girl who had climbed up one of the trees fell down and broke her arm.

Christmas

The highlight of the year was when we put on a nativity play and invited our parents to watch us perform. The older kids were allowed to play Maria, Joseph, or the angel who proclaimed "From Heaven above to earth I come," and often had to learn complicated sentences by heart. The younger kids had an easier job being the ox or the donkey since they only had to hold a mask in front of their face. The shepherds' sheep on the field only had to go "bah bah" every now and then.

The new kindergarten teacher

This Christian Christmas was over now. All kids were to be educated in the spirit of National Socialism. This new teacher had us:

>Fold our hands, bow our head
>Think of Adolf Hitler
>Who gives us our daily bread
>And protects us from danger.

That is how the new teacher's first day and my last day in kindergarten started.

When I told my parents what she had taught us, my mother wouldn't let me go anymore.

The Reichstag fire

My parents had rented out an appartement in the upper floor of our house to a teacher and his wife. She was very sad that she wasn't able to bear a child of her own and he also would have liked to have one. That is why I spent much time with them. The first ever pictures of me were taken by him. Back then, it was still very rare for someone to own a camera.

He also told me many things. For example, one time he told me about the Reichstag fire, which had happened before I was born. What I remember from that is the atrocity he told me: the Nazis themselves were the ones to set the fire.

Today, this is how I see it: Van der Lubbe was the arsonist. However, the Nazis did get wind of his plans early on. But since his plan would give them an excuse to persecute communists, they were all for it and did everything so that Van der Lubbe could carry on without any disturbance. By help of this spectacular event, Hitler was able to impose his Enabling Act and make himself a dictator for life.

9/11 World Trade Towers

Some draw a parallel between this and the attacks on the World Trade Towers on 9/11. The CIA had known about the terrorists and their plans early on and let them proceed so the US would have an excuse to invade Iraq and Afghanistan.

Reality and propaganda

My stories resonated with my English friends more than I would have thought. They, who had so far only known the Greater German Reich from Leni Riefenstahl's movies, had quite a few laughs while listening to them. Riefenstahl's big movies were "Triumph of the Will," "The Victory of Faith," and "Olympia."

The politics of the Secret Intelligence Service (2.9)

Bürgerbräukeller

"Your last story about the Reichstag fire is a good transition to the two stories I have about the Bürgerbräukeller and the incident in Venlo," Charles inserted.

Hitler was supposed to fall victim to an explosion in the Bürgerbräukeller in Munich. He regularly held speeches there in front of his most devoted followers. Usually, these gatherings lasted at least 2 hours, from 8 p.m. to 10 p.m. However, on this particular night, Hitler had to fly to Berlin earlier and left at 9 p.m. An assassin had planted a bomb within a cavity he had made in a pillar right behind Hitler's podium.

This bomb exploded on November 8, 1939 at 9:10 p.m. and cost the lives of 6 people; 50 more were injured. If Hitler hadn't left 10 minutes before that, he would have stood closest to the explosion.

A close call like that meant a huge success for propaganda since people now believed that destiny had held its protecting hand above Hitler.

Premonition or calculation?

In actual fact, the English secret service had told the German Gestapo that Elser had received 4,000 mark in Zurich to prepare an assassination attempt on Hitler.

He belonged to a communist resistance group, Agitprop, but was working on his own after the Communist Party had been outlawed. Still, he was being watched closely and his observers noticed that each night, he let himself be locked into the Bürgerbräukeller and they meticulously registered how far he had come with hollowing out the pillar each time. Each morning, he carefully covered up the evidence. On the night that Hitler held his speech, the Gestapo knew that the time fuse was set to 9:10 p.m.

Escape

It wasn't hard to guess that Elser would try to flee the country after this. That is why inconspicuous agents followed him and posts were sent to all border stations. Elser was caught on the border to Switzerland before the bomb even detonated. Residues of plaster and mortar on his clothes were something he couldn't avoid and used as evidence against him.

A question

Why didn't Hitler prevent this attempt on his life and accept that six of his followers died and 50 more were injured?

He probably thought his movement would find the most success if he were able to connect this assassination attempt to a bigger ploy that involved several of his generals. It would serve him better to bring this into court than to catch a solitary assassin before he could even carry out his attack.

Churchill wanted to keep Hitler alive at all costs. "He is our best ally. Without him, we would have no excuse in the eyes of the world to destroy Germany. We are not fighting against Hitler and the Nazis, we are fighting against the German people. It is a threat to our supremacy."

Conspiracy

A few days after the offensive in Poland, Hitler had made England a peace offer. But the offer was rejected, the reason: they didn't want to negotiate with Hitler. Since the German generals knew that a war with England would lead to a new world war, they tried everything to restore the peace that obviously was impossible for England as long as there was a Hitler. That is why they decided to have Hitler arrested and dismissed from his position. However, they wanted to make sure that England would then be ready to make peace. Canaris was insisting that Hitler shouldn't be killed, unlike Bonhoeffer in 1944.

They sent negotiators to Chamberlain. He, like most of his cabinet members, thought a war would be illogical since they all knew for certain that the British empire would not get through it unscathed.

On the condition that Hitler be unseated, an agreement would have come about.

Only Churchill was against it. He was outvoted.

Churchill's ruse

Churchill used a ruse to get his will anyway. As boss of the SIS, he established contact with the German Gestapo. They exposed the generals' plans, complete with an exhaustive list of everybody involved. The name Elser was to be found on that very list.

Clueless

Chamberlain and his cabinet members had no clue about Churchill's ruse. They would have never even thought such infamous behavior possible anyway. That is why they thought that after the assassination attempt in Bürgerbräukeller, the plan to get rid of Hitler would now be put into motion. Chamberlain therefore sent two of his negotiators across the Dutch border near Venlo the very next day to initiate contact to the conspirators.

The incident in Venlo

Someone was already waiting for them right when they crossed the border and greeted them nicely: "We were waiting for you." "This is just where you are supposed to be." "You wanted to get rid of the Führer with help of the German generals." "If I may introduce myself: Schellenberg, leader of the German Gestapo." The British negotiators had walked right into the Gestapo's open arms. They were interrogated and sent to prison right away. They only got their freedom back after the war, in May of 1945.

Unconditional surrender

And so the British secret service on the continent had completely blown its cover. That actually played into Churchill's hands perfectly. He wanted absolutely no negotiations but instead insisted on an unconditional surrender, meaning Germany should have no rights left whatsoever after its defeat. It was supposed to suffer utter destruction, just like Carthago after the 3rd Punic war. That was the historic example he had in mind.

German generals

Today, many think that the German generals had been slaves to authority, cowards, and too submissive. The events surrounding Venlo show that this is not true. So many generals were involved in the plot against Hitler that he couldn't afford to even think about punishing them all. His army would have been alone in Poland without hardly any generals. It was only in 1944, in connection to Stauffenberg's assassination attempt, that they were held accountable and executed for what they did.

However, we also have to remember men like General Paulus, who acted contrary to Hitler's orders when he surrendered to the Polish with 100,000 of his men during the hopeless battle at Stalingrad. Of course, only 10,000 of them survived captivity. Or think about Choltitz, who gave up Paris without a fight, even though Hitler had declared the city a fort, which would have lead to the city's complete destruction.

First combat actions (2.10)

In and around Gdansk

Now Houston chimed in. He had already gathered a considerable amount of details in his collection of information on the first combat actions. The official version of the surprised Polish peope being overrun completely by the Germans like a steamroller is not true at all. In actuality, the Polish had a well-prepared and optimally equipped army of 1 million soldiers at their disposal, who bravely opposed the German forces in battle. Hitler himself acknowledged the Polish heroism, expressly contradicting accounts of the world press stating that he had just blown away the Polish defences easily.

Predictions

Nobody had counted on the fact that after just a few days, the Polish forces had to retreat from Gdansk and that after 14 days, their defeat had become inevitable. Churchill himself hadn't counted on that when he had assured the Polish of his support. He had anticipated the Polish to win quickly and without even needing his military support. The first reports of daily newspapers like The Times in London or Le Monde in Paris told about the Polish cavalry's grand victories over the German attackers. These articles had been written weeks before the war had even broken out and had, as it turns out too hastily, been printed on the first day of battle. They can still be viewed in the publishers' archives.

Miscalculation

This general miscalculation isn't surprising if you consider the fact that after the Treaty of Versailles, Germany was only allowed to have 100,000 men under arms. An army smaller than that of the Czech Republic or the Netherlands. And Hitler had only had a few years to rearm his people. Poland had already taken advantage of Germany's military weakness several times. In August of 1919 and August of 1920, they had raided territories of the German Reich. They had also made plans in 1930 and 1931 to march on Berlin and conquer Schlesia. They were however never put into action because the French government had, after much consideration, decided not to participate after all.

Stalin's hesitation

Stalin also wasn't sure whether the Germans would manage to oppose the millions of Polish armed forces and emerge victorious. He therefore waited until September 17, 16 days after the war had started, to march in up to the demarcation line that had been agreed upon in the Hitler-Stalin Pact. On September 18, the different groups first met in Brest-Litowsk, which was situated on the demarcation line that was supposed to separate the spheres of influence of these two powerful nations.

Surrender in Warsaw

After 10 days, Warsaw, the capital, had to surrender. The Polish government fled the country together with 100,000 Polish fighters who wanted to continue their resistance from outside. Still, the Polish felt that England had let them down since Churchill didn't lift a finger to provide the support he had promised to give in case of an attack. His only commentary on the Russian attack was: "My support would have only been given to fight the Germans anyway."

He didn't want to get on Stalin's bad side.

Alternative facts

However, Churchill still owed Poland an explanation on why he had left them high and dry during the Russian as well as the German attack. He declared that Stalin occupying Estonia and Latvia and also conquering the East Polish territories up to the demarcation line was a huge success. With this, we have built a bulwark that will contain Hitler's lust for conquest in the East. Did he manage to pacify the Polish with this explanation? The term "alternative facts" hadn't yet been coined back then, but Churchill's distorted presentation of facts would have certainly met the definition.

Bloody Sunday

While the war ran its course in Poland, it became more and more cruel. The receding Polish soldiers had taken their revenge on Germany by massacring the population of the city Bromberg, a city mostly inhabited by Germans. This in turn lead to German soldiers taking their revenge on the Polish population.

Old-school officers that still held the values of honor and chivalry high wanted to penalize these German assaults, the pillaging, looting, and shooting. However, Hitler forbade punishment because, as he explained, he feared that the force of his army would be diminished by this during such a critical war situation.

Following the same logic, American law still suspends punishment for American soldiers as long as they are in war zones.

Drôle de Guerre (2.11)

The war in the west

Meanwhile, nothing at all happened in the west. Hitler gave orders that not one shot be fired and no one step foot on enemy territory, not even one meter, without his express command. After the Kellogg-Briand pact, defensive wars were permissable, offensive wars however were not. France, England, and Germany had all entered into this pact. If the Germans didn't attack those countries, no one would be able to denounce them as aggressors. That is why Hitler placed the utmost importance on letting them attack him first so that they would be marked as war criminals. This lead to what the British called a 'phoney war.'

Water mines

Churchill had always had a vivid imagination. He originally wanted to become a novelist. Savrola, protagonist of his first big novel, is a revolutionary hero – of course, a portrait of Churchill himself – who emerges victorious from every single fight. The name is derived from Savanarola, the name of a monk who was burned at the stake in Florence.

Drawing on his imagination, Churchill suggested throwing tens of thousands of watermines into the river Moselle above Trier on the French side. They were supposed to explode along the riparian cities with a loud bang, all the way up to Coblenz, where the Moselle flows into the Rhine. That way, the Rhenish cities would have also gotten a taste of this firework.

However, the French undermined this suggestion, fearing that some mines might make it all the way to where the Rhine flows into the Netherlands. The Dutch, rather friendly towards the Allies and officially at least neutral, would probably not be too happy about Churchill's grand idea.

Saarland

In Saarland, six villages were located outside of the German belt of defence, the Siegfried Line. They were evacuated after the Allies' declaration of war. Still, a French general could not resist and just had to at least invade those six villages. The Germans were allowed to shoot these French troops since they were invaders. This would not count as an offensive, but a defensive strike. Their general's reckless adventure cost 2,000 young French soldiers their lives.

Narvik

During a war, countries need iron and steel. The Germans only had very little of both. They got their iron ore from a Swedish mine named Kiruna. The ore was shipped from the adjacent port, Narvik. The English knew all this. Churchill, who had been appointed chief commander of the British navy when the war broke out, wanted to block the sea route from there to Germany. All Norwegian ports, Bergen, Tromsö, Hammerfest, and so on were to be mined so that German ships would not be able to sail near the shore. Instead, they would have to sail out into the open sea, where they would easily be caught and sunk by the superior English fleet.

Setback

While the English war cabinet was still discussing the matter of which English ship would be best to mine which Norwegian port, they got some news: "Hitler has already occupied the port in Narvik." Their protests of how Hitler was violating Norwegian sovereignty were all in vain now. As if the British would have asked Norwegian permission before mining their ports.

First defeat

Churchill had to spring into action. The entire British navy set sail for Narvik and was put to rout by three German ships. Incidentally, these three ships were all Germany had since they had been forced to surrender their entire imperial fleet to England after WWI. Building new ships takes time and until then, Hitler hadn't managed to build more than those three.

Scapa Flow

At that time, the German war fleet was detained in Scapa Flow. The German chief commander didn't hand the fleet over, however, and instead opted to have the entire fleet sunk. They are all still there, all those ships with their proud names, just lying on the ocean floor. It is the world's biggest ship graveyard. It got its first English addition on October 14, 1939 when a German submarine sank the Royal Oak, an English ship. It's a symbolic place.

Chamberlain resigns

People felt that chief admiral Churchill's dilettantism was so shameful that there just had to be some consequences. Neville

Chamberlain took full responsibility for his chief admiral's failures and resigned. And, oh sweet logic, who else could be his successor to the role of commander-in-chief, complete with dictatorial powers, but said genius Churchill.

Blitz (2.12)

The end of the phoney war

As soon as Berlin got wind of this, they knew that there would be no parley and no looking back with Churchill. The phoney war became a blitzkrieg. Hitler had to strike. The Battle of France on the Western Front began on May 10, 1940 and from May 27 to June 4, there were still some struggles around Dunkirk. After that, the blitzkrieg was over and the united French and British army defeated.

Blood, toil, tears, and sweat

So, at that point, Churchill had been in office only 10 days. At the beginning of his inauguration, he had held his famous speech, "I have nothing to offer but blood, toil, tears, and sweat." Two weeks later, he had once again put his genius commanding skills to the test.

Black dog

Churchill admits that Hitler won. "But his generals' stupidity has cost him the ultimate victory." They had neglected to capture the defeated English soldiers. That was Churchill's opinion. If they had done so, the war would have been over since the English politicians, keen on peace, would have no longer let Churchill dictate the war's continuation.

Misdirection?

It is unclear to us whether Churchill said this in an attempt to consciously misdirect people or whether he really didn't know that the German generals had indeed started to capture the English soldiers, but that Hitler had then personally prevented them from actually imprisoning them. He had consciously allowed the English to flee, thinking that if he spared the English soldiers the humiliation of being captured and didn't hurt their pride, the members of the English government that were affable to him would be more inclined to want peace. However, that plan definitely didn't pan out.

Rescue

300,000 British soldiers were able to save themselves and return to England by crossing this narrow point of the canal with boats. 85,000 French soldiers also managed to cross over to England. Any material both armies had had was left behind to rot. Among it were the arms that Onassis had spent so many years transporting. The soldiers had only one week to return to safety, from May 27 to June 4, 1940.

Without a fight

10 days later, the German troops took over Paris without a fight while the majority of the defeated French troops retreated in the general direction of Bordeaux. The leading general ordering this retreat and also deciding to stand down without further battles was Maréchal Pétain, by then already 84 years old and the big hero of Verdun during WWI.

Surrender

On June 22, 1940, he agreed to surrender in Compiégne, in the same historic railway car where the shameful Treaty of Versailles had been signed. It was decided that the North of France would henceforth be placed under German administration. The South of France was to keep an independent French government. However, the provisional French government was to be transferred to Vichy because the coastlines along the canal and the Atlantic were occupied and fortified to strengthen the defences. Pétain was to be France's new president.

Collaboration

A collaboration with the Germans was necessary in order to provide for the Southern population, to keep up commerce, and basically to lead any kind of life as a nation. Still, Pétain firmly rejected Hitler's wish that France would now become a German ally in the fight against England. Pétain wanted to remain neutral. Nonetheless, he did keep his army and his entire undamaged war fleet, the biggest fleet following England's. These forces were supposed to guarantee Vichy-

France's control over its colonies in Algeria, Morocco, and Tunesia. In addition, Hitler released 2 million French soldiers from captivity.

Paris

Hitler wanted to ensure France's benevolence. After the end of the war, France was supposed to be restored with its old borders – only Alsace-Lorraine was going to stay German territory. The German occupation of Paris was not meant to disturb its cultural life. Many great French artists and actors were able to continue their careers: Cocteau, Max, Ophüls, Jean Marais, Giraudoux, Anouilh, and many others provided sophisticated entertainment in the French capital. For the German occupying forces, being delegated to Paris was a privilege. Champagne and exquisite French wines, both of which were available in large amounts, turned almost every day into a party.

Pétain

Pétain and many of those working with him were attacked in the most shocking ways after the war. The by then 89-year-old was even sentenced to death because he wouldn't continue fighting and had even collaborated with the enemy. However, Général de Gaulle commuted his death sentence to life imprisonment.

Général de Gaulle

De Gaulle himself chose a path different from Pétain's. Together with all other generals, he was in Bordeaux when he heard that 85,000 French soldiers had been able to flee to

England. Since he was carrying the entire war chest, he decided and managed to relocate to England with those funds. Once there, he made the French soldiers swear an oath to him and declared this a government in exile. 4 days later, on June 22, 1940, Pétain surrendered. Detractors claim this was partly due to him having no money left since de Gaulle had taken it all with him to England.

We are not alone

At first, Churchill was very pleased by this reinforcement. He even entrusted de Gaulle with a piece of information that was still top secret: the situation was far from hopeless since FDR had long since promised to enter the war and had systematically worked towards it since 1932 – and his preparations were almost done. However, this information was to be kept an absolute secret. Even in Washington, only select members of the government were in on it. So, naturally, de Gaulle wasn't allowed to give any information on the topic during his radio speech. He was only allowed to say "We are not alone," meaning that backup and help would come. Who would provide them? Well, that was easy enough to guess.

The obligation to stay informed

An interesting exchange between FDR and one of his ministers in Congress is passed down. After the president had informed the USA of the impending entry into the war and that each year, billions of dollars had already been invested in this cause, one minister criticized him for doing all this without informing his parliament. Not one of the members of government had known about his plan. FDR's answer was: "I have to reprimand you severely. As a member of this government, you are obligated to stay informed about everything that is going on."

Only, how was the minister supposed to fulfill his obligation when the whole thing was kept top secret?
Since the beginning of the First World War, politics in the USA are no longer ruled by the elected government but exclusively by the Secret Service.

Yemen

The current drone attacks in Yemen that cost more than 3,000 lives each year (that means about 10 murders a day!) take place without the Senate or the Congress debating the targets or purpose of the attacks. Only now and then do we hear that something has gone terribly wrong, like for example a wedding party with 150 civilians being hit and killed by accident.

French government in exile (2.13)

Atrocities

The crucial question was: When will the USA enter the war? The American population as a whole was against participation in European wars. That is why FDR needed to present some kind of atrocity that would cause such an uproar amongst his people that it would then be ready to enter the war. Various fake news segments were initiated. But their effectiveness was called into doubt. Walt Disney was supposed to make an animated movie that illustrated how Hitler eats a well-fed infant each morning for breakfast. But since he had been mocked for being a vegetarian shortly before, that didn't seem like a good idea. Another idea was to show how SS soldiers cut open pregnant women, grill their embryos on their campfires, and eat them as a delicacy. That idea was also rejected because SS soldiers should rather be shown as unkempt savages that devour wild boars raw than as lovers of extravagant delicacies.

Eugenics

At that point, actual atrocities were already taking place in Germany under the euphemistic name euthanasia, in this case meaning "mercy killings" of genetically predisposed disabled people. Even in Germany, this was met with widespread protests. However, it was not seen as enough of a reason to enter the war because, in fact, the first internationally recognized scientists for eugenics came from the US. The science of the Prevention of Genetically Diseased Offspring had its roots there.

Anti-Jewish laws

The laws prohibiting marriages between Aryans and Jews and other races as well had been supported by many Orthodox Jews. In order to protect their distinct identity, they didn't want mixed marriages. People even say that Hitler had to promise Rothschild to pass these laws in return for his help financing the election campaign. Unto this day, no Jew in Israel is allowed to marry someone of non-Jewish faith. There is no registry office, only a rabbi is entitled to marry couples. If the prospective partners don't meet the requirements, they have to get married outside of the country, the closest location being Cyprus. However, Israel does recognize the marriage afterwards.

Mers-el-Kebir

De Gaulle's solidarity with Churchill was really put to the test when the latter had the French fleet in Mers-el-Kebir attacked and sunk by plane. This fleet was supposed to guarantee Vichy-France's dominance in its African colonies. Churchill however felt that Hitler might use this big war fleet to his advantage in the fight against England – in all probability, a needless concern. All Churchill did was break international law by sinking the fleet of a country that wasn't at war with England, costing the lives of 1,300 French seamen.

De Gaulle couldn't just accept that without protest. "That was a war crime," he said to Churchill. Of course, Churchill laughed and answered: "As soon as I've won, it won't be a war crime anymore." And then he added: "If you keep reproaching me, I will have you liquidated." Churchill was very proud of his

French proficiency, which is why he even said that last part in French: "Si vous m'obstaclerez je vous liquiderai." Obstacle in the sense of obstruction is an actual French word; obstacler, putting obstacles in someone's way, however is not. Churchill was being linguistically creative.

Fillet piece

They had other controversial issues as well. FDR had heard that the most precious piece of land France had in Indochina was Vietnam: a country with an intelligent and rich population, lots of profit to be made. He asked Churchill, wouldn't it be smart to get our hands on that piece of colonial territory now? I heard de Gaulle is staying with you in London. Couldn't you just have him eliminated? Churchill answered: "At the moment, he has 85,000 French men under oath, but I'm sure we will get our chance after the war."

FDR's son

A letter from FDR's son confirmed that his father was very worried by how badly the Vietnamese were treated by the French. And that he would have liked to take the country over for a few years so that it could be prepared for democratic development. The same held true for all English colonies. Roosevelt wanted to put them all under US administration because he thought the American government would be better qualified for this than the English government.

Churchill's interpretation

He presented FDR's intentions as truly positive. According to him, there was no plan of a hostile takeover, instead, it would have been an equal union of these two powerful nations.

Imbalance

Little Fat Man Churchill and almost-two-meter giant de Gaulle grew apart more and more. They just weren't compatible. De Gaulle was a distinguished, educated man while Churchill was not sophisticated at all. When he was introduced to Greta Garbo, the Unapproachable, the Divine, the Diva, he grabbed her breasts in front of the camera. He didn't understand why people were so upset by it. I only wanted to check if they were real.

When he was served a refined dry Riesling in the Dolder, Zurich's posh restaurant, nobody knew that Churchill preferred sweet port and full-bodied French Bordeaux. He thought the white wine was so sour that without much ado, he spat it into the plate of the lady sitting next to him. Once again, he didn't understand the ensuing excitement, after all, they had brought her a fresh plate right away. That is why the English called him guttersnipe.

X-Day

He excluded de Gaulle from all political decisions. The latter was only informed of the plans to have the Allies' forces land in Brittany the evening before it happened. While bombing the French coastal cities, no consideration was shown for French civilians. The complete destruction of St. Malo, the beautiful city Caen, or even the metropolis Marseille, executed under the pretense of German soldiers supposedly being holed up there, was completely unjustified.

Casablanca

The forceful invasion of Morocco and the conquest of Casablanca were against international law. In those territories, the administration of the neutral Vichy-government still prevailed. However, fights with government-loyal Frenchmen were over soon thanks to the superior strength of the British and American forces. "Just" a few hundred French soldiers lost their lives and Churchill was able to hold the Casablanca Conference with FDR and start the North African campaign from there.

After the war (2.14)

Victory parade

Churchill had imagined a triumphant intrusion into the French capital, Paris. He himself and his troops would be in the front rows, followed by the Americans, the Polish, and the rear would be brought up by de Gaulle and his French troops.

Battle of Paris

He had really been looking forward to the Battle of Paris, during which he could have laid waste to the city's magnificent buildings. However, his plans were foiled by General Choltitz, who opposed Hitler's commands and gave the city up without a fight.

Entry

De Gaulle used this opportunity and was the first to enter the city with his French troops while Churchill was still busy planning his victory parade.

De Gaulle therefore also had the chance to prevent communist underground fighters, whose headquarters were in the Renault car factories, from declaring Paris a Soviet republic based on Stalin's example.

Prostitutes

Churchill always had the secret service tell him the current jokes that were circulating in the territories they were spying out. When he heard the following joke, in which two prostitutes complain because their business is low, he figured that if the German soldiers didn't want to hump anymore, then their morale had to also be low. Now is the time to attack. And now for the joke: One prostitute says to the other: "Today, I had to give it up for a piece of bread…" The other one replies: "And I did it so I'd finally get something warm in my belly."

The women who had gotten involved with Germans were treated very badly after the war. Their hair was cut off, they were herded through the streets, and many of them were shot. A very eloquent lady of pleasure who was tried for having relations with Germans excused herself by pointing out "mon cul est international" (my ass is international).
But even this worldly lady was herded through the streets with her hair shaved off.

Separation (2.15)

A separate path

De Gaulle wanted to get away from England and the USA. He wanted a Europe that consisted of native countries and excluded England. That country had, in his eyes, become an American cohort and didn't belong to Europe. France also didn't join NATO and de Gaulle attached great importance to France building its own nuclear bomb so it would not be dependent on the USA and England. This weapon was mockingly called "force de frappe" to make it sound cuter.

German-French friendship

De Gaulle knew that the two countries were actually sister nations. Just like Charlemagne's descendants, who at first were kings of the Eastern and Western realms before unfortunately becoming bitter enemies in the 19th century. In Ludwigsburg, he held a speech in German that triggered town twinning and student exchanges between German and French schools. He called out to German adolescents, telling them "you are the children of a great civilized nation and you can be proud to be a part of it." That was the exact opposite of what the English and the Americans were doing, blaming the Germans for everything, calling it their collective guilt.

The German government had to promise America right away that their friendship would, of course, have priority. The USA didn't like seeing those two nations so close.

Appraisal

When considering the political events that took place during those years retrospectively, a different evaluation of Pétain's role becomes necessary. He was taken captive and sentenced to death when actually, his surrender had saved the French cities from being destroyed. Also, 250,000 war casualties is a very small number compared to 27 million dead Russian and 6 million dead Polish soldiers. France should in fact be very grateful to him.

When Mitterand placed a white rose on Pétain's grave on the Atlantic island the old man had been banished to, he almost had to resign from presidency. This proves that France also hasn't yet gotten over the war hysteria.

Goodbye

While we were telling all these stories that didn't end with the war, it had gotten late, midnight was already long gone. Cynthia and Charles said goodbye and Douglas also took a taxi home. We agreed that we should meet again soon for another night of conversation. I stayed overnight at Houston's and on the next day, we took a cruise on the River Thames, despite not getting much sleep.

The 3rd day

A cruise on the River Thames (3.1)

St. Paul's

Such a cruise is always a worthwhile experience. Close to the Tower Bridge, we went aboard one of the boats that travel up and down the river at regular intervals and rode upstream. It is superb how well modern buildings and skyscrapers are incorporated into the historic city. The Shard, the Swiss Re Tower, Gherkin, as well as the London Eye.

However, there are some problems. The elegantly curved façade of one building complex made of glass has the same effect a giant burning lense would have. The sunlight is collected, causing the concentrated beam to burn holes into the metal of parked cars. The really unsuitable giant black carpet in front of the façade doesn't seem like a permanent solution.

Right after we had started our boat ride, the big dome of St. Paul's cathedral appeared on our right. The location had previously been the site of an older church. The cathedral had been built by famous architect Christopher Wren after the Great Fire of London. In its crypt, hundreds of tombs have been built for national war heroes.

Any Englishman is proud of the many wars England has fought in. Even Houston was excitedly telling me that there is no country on Earth that has fought as many wars as England.

Still, since their foundation and the war of independence, the USA are slowly gaining on the Brits. During the last 20 years, the United States have made 1,200 military interventions in different regions all over the world.

„And how's Germany doing on that list?" I asked. Not even close. Your country, so proud of its brave soldiers, is really far behind. It pretty much takes last place on that list.

Switzerland

There are only two countries that we have never waged war on: Mongolia and Switzerland. We were simply not interested in Mongolia, since natural resources have only been discovered there over the last few years. Switzerland however? There would have been a lot to gain there. And then something happened that came as a surprise to me: Houston was criticizing this country for never letting the English conduct a raid there. Furthermore, he said that the enormous amounts of money the potentates from all over the world deposit on Swiss bank accounts would be much better embezzled by the Bank of England.

You're not being serious right now. You're a satyr in disguise. Whatever. A collection of stories is none the worse for containing some satire.

A stray missile

We were still looking at St. Paul's cathedral when Houston remembered that during the German attacks on the docks, a stray missile had hit the cathedral. Pictures from that time show how much debris can be caused by just one hit.

He also told me that Churchill had talked to common Londoners and was very impressed by the psychological impact of having such a symbolic building destroyed. He realized that people are more devastated if big national monuments are destroyed than if it is just private buildings and industrial plants.

Churchill drew a simple conclusion: Before lift-off, he told his pilots they should preferably aim their missiles at prominent buildings like cathedrals, domes, churches, and castles.

Krönungskapelle

The Krönungskapelle (coronation chapel) in Aachen was supposed to be the first target. It was built on behalf of Charlemagne around 800, the same year that saw the construction of the Dome of the rock in Jerusalem, which has a similar architectural style. Today, it is a World Heritage Site. Since every man fit for military service was serving on the frontlines, some 16-year-old high school students had volunteered to protect the chapel. During air raids, they would not seek refuge in bomb shelters and instead remove dangerous incendiary bombs that were a threat to the old and dry woodwork.

Twice more, Churchill gave orders to have this monument to the coronation of German kings and emperors destroyed. Luckily, to no avail.

Cologne Cathedral

Furthermore, it was of the utmost importance to Churchill that the Cologne Cathedral be laid to waste. The cathedral is a national monument for every German. All federal German states supported the completion of the cathedral in the 19th century. The dome was supposed to show that Christian faith will live on in Germany even after the anticlerical French Revolution.

It is truly surprising that this monument has survived 70 hits.

Vienna

When the air raids extended to the South and into Austria, Churchill reminded the pilots that were bombing the city that they should definitely destroy the Opera House and St. Stephen's Cathedral. Which they managed to do. The Opera House was Vienna's symbol as world capital of music and famous Mozart operas premiered there. St. Stephen's Cathedral saw the coronation of the Hapsburg emperors.

Strasbourg Cathedral

Hitler rated this building a national monument to German architecture. Goethe had studied in Strasbourg and written about its architect, Erwin von Steinbach. Since Strasbourg wasn't situated within the battle zone and was inhabited exclusively by the French when the war started, Churchill only saw a chance to have this monument destroyed in the spring of 1945. At that point, German soldiers were fleeing to Southern Germany and passing through Strasbourg when the western front retreated. The damages to the cathedral were dreadful and it took the French 20 years before they could start picking up the pieces. For Churchill, it was a way of pretending the bombs had been meant for the fleeing soldiers.

Globe Theatre

To our left, the Globe Theatre came into view, Shakespeare's stage. Churchill claimed that he knew every one of his plays by heart. He did have a phenomenal memory and took a great liking to Shakespeare's plays. He felt that with Shakespeare, you could finally tell when a play was over – when everybody was lying dead on the stage. That really suited his killer instinct.

Tin soldiers

Because Churchill was suffering from Dyscalculia and practicing maths with him was pointless, his private teacher instead played out all of world history's great battles with a big collection of tin soldiers. The Battle of Waterloo with Wellington, the ocean battle of Trafalgar, the battles of Cesar and Alexander the Great. And the battle was never over until every last tin soldier on both sides had fallen down.

Dad's opinion

Churchill's father sometimes came to watch them play with the tin soldiers. Churchill's comment on that was: "He had recognized my military genius early on, which is why he sent me to the Royal Military Academy Sandhurst."

Later on, he put this praise into perspective: „While watching me play with my tin soldiers, he had accepted early on that sending me to study in Oxford was out of the question."

Savoy Hotel

It may well be London's most elegant hotel and it certainly is enormously big. It is a place where memories are made, and many celebrities have spent a night there. Its rooftops and upper floors appeared to our right.
Houston told me which celebrities had stayed there. I was mainly interested in Herbert Hoover, who had taken money out of his own pocket during WWI and had given it to the American guests stranded there. They had been staying in Europe and were surprised by the outbreak of the war. They weren't able to return to America right away, but also didn't have enough money to stay much longer. Hoover also asked his friends to use their private funds to help them out. The stranded Americans behaved very honorably and later sent all of the money back, except for 400 dollars.

Aid campaign

Soon afterwards, Hoover started a big campaign. Due to the Germans marching through and the military operations of WWI, alimentary care for the entire Belgian population had collapsed. Martial law states that the occupants of a country have to provide for its population. However, Emperor Wilhelm wasn't able to do that in this difficult situation. Especially the naval blockade Churchill had ordered made it impossible to reach any Belgian port. And so Hoover obtained the right to pass enemy lines with a white flag, meaning he wasn't attacked and could reach a Dutch port so that Belgium could be provided with food.

The German emperor was more than happy to agree to this, but Churchill was furious. His arguments were these: "If Belgian people starve, it's a war crime that the German emperor can be accused of and I would really like to have him hanged." Even though Belgium was an English ally, Churchill would have rather seen its population die than have Hoover successfully carry out his aid campaign.

Hoover was the person Churchill hated most. "I hate him even more than I hate Hitler." I will tell you more about this animosity later, said Houston.

The Big Mississippi Flood of 1927

The biggest flood of all times. 70,000 square kilometers were covered 9 meters deep in water. The flood victims had nothing but the wet clothes on their backs. So, Hoover simply took money out of his own pocket again so they would be able to buy some food over the next few days.

Today, a state of catastrophe emergency is declared, the governor makes his rounds and promises help in the foreseeable future, and the victims can sometimes wait for it for months.

Presidential election

It was his initiative in situations like these that made the American population put their trust in Hoover. In the following year, he was elected US president, even though the entire press was spreading smear campaigns and lies about him.

Some parallels

Today, we see astonishingly parallel events take place. The American population, acting against the will of the establishment, has elected Trump and not Hillary Clinton, despite all contrary newspaper propaganda.

A billion dollars, spent by the richest banks in support of Hillary's election campaign, all in vain. It is a sign that the press is not yet omnipotent because more and more people recognize that they are fed lies.

Nancy Astor (3.2)

Waldorf Astoria

Another elegant, distinguished hotel close to the Royal Opera in London is the Waldorf Astoria. We could see its roof from our boat. The eponymous hotel in New York belongs to the same man. His wife is Nancy Astor. She was the first female delegate of the British parliament. Churchill, misogynist that he was, sneered at that and said, "in parliament, he now felt like someone sitting naked in his bathtub and being surprised by an unsolicited intruder."

Change of parties

The two clashed right away. As an aristocrat, Churchill naturally was a member of the Conservative Party, the same party Nancy Astor belonged to. This party protected the interests of wealthy people. Prohibitive taxes were supposed to guarantee higher profits for them. He was assigned an election district where the Labour Party had a majority. That meant that his chances of being elected were close to zero. So, he changed sides and joined the Labour Party. Now, he was allowed to run in an election district where he was sure to be elected. Suddenly, he was campaigning for free trade, which would mean cheaper products for the poorer population. "The main thing is that I can serve my country" is how he explained this decision.

Nancy thought his behavior was spineless and told him: "If I was your wife, I would poison your tea." Churchill replied: "Dear Nancy, if I were your husband, I'd drink it."

In my opinion, Churchill's best witticism.

Masked ball

During a masked ball, Churchill dressed up with a black blindfold and one arm in a sling, imitating his big idol Nelson. Nancy came over to him and said: "You can wear whatever disguise you want, people still recognize you right away. Should you be sober for once, now then people wouldn't think it was you." Even quick-witted Churchill was momentarily stumped by that and didn't know how to answer.

Lord Nelson's last love

There is a movie, starring Vivian Leigh, that resonated so well with Churchill that he was moved to tears each time he watched it, which he did 20 times. He saw himself in this story that showed Nelson's lover, Lady Hamilton, struggling to survive after his death had left her penniless, forced to beg and steal. To Churchill, this movie was a perfect example of perseverance in a desperate situation. At that moment, it served as an example for the whole nation to not give up after being defeated in the Battle of Dunkirk. Churchill found this movie to be a piece of art, equal to one of Shakespeare's plays and proof that war, the father of everything, motivated people to do their very best, even artists.

Yet again

Only a few days after the masked ball, Nancy and Winston had yet another quarrel in parliament. Nancy accused him: "And once again, you are drunk." Churchill's response: "Now, you listen to me, Nancy. I am drunk. But when I wake up tomorrow, I will be sober again. You, my dear, are ugly and when you look into your mirror tomorrow, you will still be as ugly as today." Not at all gentlemanlike. From that point on, the two of them left each other alone.

Unrequited love

Churchill later explained their animosity by saying: "She would have liked to marry me, but since I was already married, she felt rejected."
While this explanation is typical for Churchill, it certainly contains not one ounce of truth. Nancy Astor was a very beautiful, elegant woman. Pictures of her can easily be found on Google. Furthermore, her super-rich husband, who owned both world class hotels, was far more handsome than the quite unattractive Winston Churchill.

City of London

By then, our boat had sailed along the entire length of the waterside promenade of the City of London. It is a mile in length and in width and practically the center of the cosmopolitan city. Not everybody knows that this square mile belongs to the private estate of Baron von Rothschild. It's the financial center of the world. During the day, hundreds of thousands of people come here to work; by night, only the few thousand who have the privilege to live there stay. Unlike the Vatican, the City of London is not governed as an autonomous state, it does however have its own laws, security personnel, and administration. Even the Queen would not be allowed to officially enter without announcing her visit beforehand. The Bank of England, supposedly the kingdom's national bank, is in actual fact a private Rothschild bank. The Temple Church and other temples, law schools, the Old Bailey, etc. etc. also belong to this estate.

Westminster Abbey (3.3)

Westminster

Westminster is located on the immediate eastern border of the City of London. Everybody knows the magnificent parliament building and the bell tower, Big Ben. This is where we got off the boat and crossed the street to get to thousand-year-old Westminster Abbey. It was built by William the Conqueror and he was coronated there. Ever since then, it has been the impressive backdrop to all important state ceremonies and it still is nowadays. Grand memorial services, coronations, and weddings are held there, the last big event being Prince William and Kate's wedding.

Elisabeth's tomb

We got some audio guides (what a wonderful invention!), but Houston was still able to explain everything much better. We paused for a while at the tomb of Elisabeth I. Its design is marvelous. It is just a few meters away from Mary Stewart's tomb, which is just as magnificent and has the same design. Mary Stewart's son, Jakob I, had it built for her and made sure that it was in no way inferior to the tomb of the queen who had had his mother beheaded.

Mary Stewart

She was the queen of Scotland, but she had to flee because she had asked her stableboy to place a bomb under her husband's bed. Her Scottish subjects resented her for it. Unfortunately, she ended up in England. It was unfortunate because in the eyes of the catholic world, protestant Elisabeth wasn't the rightful queen. Elisabeth had come from Henry VIII's marriage with Anne Boleyn, a marriage the Pope didn't recognize. From a catholic point of view, Mary Stewart was the first in line to the throne since any descendants from Henry's later marriages were also out of the question, naturally.

Assassination attempts

Mary Stewart's followers therefore tried to get rid of Queen Elisabeth I by assassinating her, so that catholic Mary Stewart could ascend the throne. The tensions between them and the attempts on her life caused Elisabeth to go to court against Mary Stewart, which resulted in the Scottish queen's death at the hands of an executioner.

Tragic irony

The ironic thing was that Elisabeth had no children of her own. So, she had no choice but to appoint her rival's son as her successor. She never married and was called the Virgin Queen. However, the word about her numerous affairs, particularly with the great pirate Sir Walter Raleigh and Francis Drake, did get out. That is why Raleigh called the colony on the East Coast of America that he conquered Virginia – virgin land. Perhaps he meant it ironically.

A crazy theory

Houston offers a pretty incredible explanation for Elisabeth's biography. He said: "Elisabeth wasn't female, she was a man. She always wore clothes with high-necked ruffles so people wouldn't see her Adam's apple. The stubble on her chin was covered with thick white makeup." That would mean she was not a virgin but a gay.

Explanation

Houston could even explain how he had gotten to believe such a thing. He elaborated that after her mother's execution, Henry VIII completely neglected his daughter, didn't care for her ever again and that monks raised her instead. When Mary, the catholic heir apparent from Henry's first marriage, died, a new heir had to be found. Since the young girl had been so neglected, it had died soon after reaching the monastery and now the monks were afraid of the king's wrath. So, they dressed up a young boy around Elisabeth's age in girls' clothes and apparently, the boy played his role until the end.

Pegasus

The story made me laugh, but then I still told Houston that this probably wasn't the Pegasus of stories, it rather resembled a billy goat instead.

Armada

In any case, it is beyond dispute that due credit has to be given to this great queen for everything she accomplished politically. She turned England into a world power. Philipp II, who sent his big armada to England to bring the queen to justice for having Mary Stewart beheaded, suffered his greatest defeat.

The actual reason for this military conflict was that English pirates were robbing Spanish ships that were filled with gold from the newfound American continent. The Spanish king wanted to put an end to this.

Francis Drake

He was the greatest pirate and most successful buccaneer of all times. Nobody brought Elisabeth more gold than he did. His clever trick was to not attack Spanish ships in the Atlantic where they had built their defenses but instead wait until they had reached the Pacific and weren't counting on being assaulted. Houston and I were planning to go see his Golden Hinde, which lies at anchor on the River Thames. Sadly, it's not the original ship but only a replica.

It practically goes without saying that Francis Drake was knighted by Elisabeth I.

Incidentally, he was the first seaman to sail around the world and make it out alive. He had to take the western sea route past India and the southern tip of Africa to bring the stolen gold to England.

As we know, Magellan made it half way before he was eaten by indigenous people on the island Cebu. Only one of his ships reached Portugal.

Jakob I

However, Mary Stewart's son and Elisabeth's successor was never well liked by his people, and with his son, Carolus

Stuardus, it was even worse. His life was also ended by decapitation. This time, Cromwell was the executioner. Apparently, the English are very industrious when it comes to taking people's heads off. Long before the French followed suit during the French Revolution when they beheaded Mary Antoinette and Louis XVI, the English had already perfected it.

Poets' Corner

Westminster's nave is rounded off with a memorial corner the English have set up for their great poets and musicians. Busts and commemorative plaques remind people of those great artists. It's very moving and triggers many memories. There is also a bust of Händel that commemorates his life and work in London. His Halleluja from his oratorio Messiah will forever remain unforgotten. Naturally, there is also a statue of Shakespeare, whose sonnets are equal to his great plays. A plaquet is embedded in the floor for Dickens, the author of the unforgettable novel David Copperfield. But many others like Chaucer and his Canterbury Tales, more skilfull than the Decameron, are commemorated here. Thomas Morus and Utopia, Thackeray and vanity fair. Lord Byron, Yeats, Keats, they all can be found here. With just a few short words, Wordsworth uses his poems, "a host of golden daffodils," to evoke the magic of springtime when the island's meadows are filled with daffodils and primroses.
I just wish we had a memorial corner like that in Germany.

German-English friendship

The close-knit literary and cultural connections between Germany and England started during Goethe's lifetime with the literary perception of Shakespeare. Why not take this as an incentive to form a close German-British friendship, similar to the German-French friendship, which has allowed for valuable relationships? After all, the German preference for English novelists, most of all, perseveres until today.

War rooms (3.4)

Parliament Square

The Poets' Corner marks the end of the tour of the cathedral. We gave back our audio guides and crossed Parliament Square by foot, passing the Churchill Statue, until we reached the war rooms. Their entrance is located at the rear side of the Treasury. Churchill's memorial was placed between Parliament and the command center from which he had directed the Second World War.

Churchill's bronze statue

The "little fat man", as he was called, is draped in an oversized general's coat. His facial expression is strong and right on – everybody can recognize him instantly, even without his cigar. He is pictured as the one who defeated the "greatest commander of all times," which, in Germany, has taken an ironic meaning and become a derogatory name for Adolf Hitler. However, everyone knows that England had been completely dependent on US intervention, just like France had been, in both World Wars, and that it is only thanks to the USA that those countries emerged victorious.

Sudeten crisis

In early 1938, the war rooms had been built as bunkers for the war government during the war on Germany that was thought to be imminent due to the Sudeten crisis. Three meters of concrete separate the ground floor from the two lower levels. This was thought to provide optimal security for the bombs that were used back then.

Baruch

The „King of Wallstreet," who had become one of the richest men alive thanks to speculating on the stock market, advised his friend Churchill that now was the time to buy war bonds. Churchill even took out a million pound loan for this. However, the bonds became worthless after the surprise peace agreement in Munich. Churchill was completely broke. He couldn't even pay the interest rates on his loan and there was talk of his private house in Chartwell being mortgaged.

Critical of the agreement

Keeping this in mind, you can suddenly see Churchill's fierce criticism of the agreement in a different light. The population of Paris and London however was overjoyed that a war had been averted.

Profit

That's understandable if you consider that all that common people get out of a war is blood, sweat, and tears. If the war had actually broken out, Churchill would have added another witticism to his famous "I have nothing to offer but blood, toil, tears, and sweat" speech. He wanted to say: "but my friend Baruch and I are really going to make a killing."

The English are known for their morbid humor. Still, it is pretty doubtful that they would have been very amused by that particular punchline.

Strakosch

Obviously, Baruch had to compensate for Churchill's financial catastrophe. He asked Strakosch, a rich Viennese Jew, to cover his friend's millions of debt and take over the now worthless war bonds. Strakosch had no trouble doing so and when the war broke out a year later, God bless, Strakosch's reward for his merciful act was thousandfold because the value of war bonds now increased tremendously.

Entrance

Many visitors were already waiting to enter the war rooms and so we had a look at the close-by St. James Park, a particularly beautiful spot. In the distance, you can see Buckingham Palace through the leaves and branches of the trees. Afterwards, we joined the waiting line and suffered an especially thorough examination by security. Well, obviously, since an attack on this historic place would have a special symbolic power.

There had already been quite the commotion when Churchill's statue had been defiled. It had been smeared with swastikas,

110

covered in crap, and urinated on. Another problem was caused by the pigeons that sat on the statue's head and made Churchill's face drip with their white excrements. However, a solution was found for this. The metal is live at all times, preventing the pidgeons from sitting on it. Originally, people had been thinking about wrapping Churchill's head in thorns and barbed wire, but this idea was doffed because of the similarity to crucified Jesus's crown of thorns.

Conference hall

The first room you pass is a small hall where Churchill and his war cabinet had held meetings. All in all, the war rooms don't exactly burst with luxury. If you then consider the many heavy smokers (Churchill never once took the cigar out of his mouth) all gathered in one room without air condition, you can imagine that the five war years spent in these rooms certainly weren't a lot of fun.

Toilet

The left rear door is the kind of prominent, airtight door you might find in cold-storage rooms. What's more, it is completely soundproof. It is the door that leads to Churchill's private toilet and nobody but him was allowed to go in. Still, it must have been kind of strange to see Churchill urgently run to the public toilet after having spent hours on end in his private toilet. The explanation: His 'private toilet' was actually the hermetically sealed room that contained the broadcasting station connecting him directly to FDR. Only Churchill was allowed to use it. In fear of decoding spies, this connection had its own secret language. Churchill and Roosevelt were certain that the Germans had never been able to crack this particular code. However, there are reports that indicate that the Germans did manage to crack it.

Enigma

The Germans had developed an encryption code that still cannot technically be outdone unto this day – Enigma. However, defying all probability, a genius Englishman managed to do what no one had thought possible. He cracked the code and now, all secret messages the Germans were exchanging with their general staff and allies were decrypted. This Englishman's tragic fate, caused by structuralized homophobia, is appalling.

The only secret language that was never decrypted was American. They had the idea to use a Hopi Indian dialect for communication. In order to decrypt their messages, a large amount of time would have been necessary, probably comparable to Champollion's decyphering of the hieroglyphs.

Kitchen and bedroom

The kitchen is also very frugal and equipped with cheap cooking utensils. It was meant for Churchill and him alone. The cook only prepared his food. Because Churchill was afraid of being poisoned, no one was allowed to be in the same room with him or, God forbid, join his meal. The bedroom with its single bed is squallid. Clementine, Winston's wife, had to stay at their private house in Chartwell. Quite the big sacrifice for a man who held luxury above all else.

Card rooms (3.5)

Global maps

Giant wall maps were suspended in stands and the movement of the front lines was documented on them with pins. Churchill then informed his friend Franklin as well as he could, seeing as Franklin was absolutely clueless when it came to geography. Incidentally, this is typical for all American politicians. Like the rest of their people, they live in splendid isolation.

San Diego

Without Churchill's help, FDR would have never managed to provoke Japan to strike first. The American flying tigers were inflicting serious damage, sinking hundreds of Japanese ships, but no matter how much he kept increasing their casualties, the Japanese just endured it. It all changed only after Churchill pointed out that the Japanese had to stay passive because they weren't actually able to strike against the USA. Their planes couldn't reach the continent, where the entire Pacific fleet was based in San Diego. First, Roosevelt had to move this fleet to Hawaii. From there, it was half way to Japan. The American Secret Service leaked the information. Only now had the "day of ignominy" become possible. Churchill rejoiced because now he officially had the Americans on his side in his fight against Germany.

Aircraft carrier

The Americans realized that in a modern war, it was no longer ships that decided the outcome, not even reinforced armored cruisers did the trick anymore. Planes are faster and a normal ship can indeed be sunk by bombs. And so FDR was able to sacrifice the entire outdated Pacific fleet and use it as bait. Of course, not without stationing his four modern aircraft carriers closer to Japan the night before. They were moved to the Midway Islands, making it possible to start bombarding Japanese cities in the days right after the war had been declared.

Arizona

Shocking human fates were triggered by the destruction of the Pacific fleet. The ship Arizona tilted, parts of it still rising above water. 1,300 mariners were trapped in their cabins and rescue teams weren't able to help them. The death throes of the soldiers trapped in the hull of the ship lasted days.

Second wave of attacks

Then, the Japanese initiated their second wave of attacks. All planes on the airport in Honolulu were destroyed before the pilots were even able to start their engines. Plans for a third wave of attacks on the fuel tanks were made, but then cancelled because the Japanese felt that they had done enough damage to force the Americans into peace negotiations. That was their one big mistake. If the fuel had been destroyed, it would have taken the US many weeks to replace it. But as it was, Roosevelt could retaliate right away.

Tokyo

Due to the many earthquakes, Japanese cities are mostly filled with one-storey houses made of wood. The planes flying on

114

Tokyo mostly used incendiary bombs and caused a firestorm of hurricane force. It cost more than 100,000 lives. Only few westerners even know about the bomb attacks on all big Japanese cities and about the horrific number of people that died because of them.

Genocide

Right from the get-go, the war on Japan was focused on killing civilians. Japan's main four islands are all volcanic. They have no natural resources, making them worthless from an American point of view. The Japanese population however is hardworking and intelligent. They are a fierce competition in the economic battle. And so the USA had no interest in leaving those four islands populated.

Churchill's call

Logically, Churchill called for all soldiers to: "Kill them all. Men, women, children. The healthy and the sick. Why not bomb a hospital? The wounded in there will only be nursed back to health and might fight us again later."

This demand really complements his previous orders: "The German race is to be exterminated completely."

Declaration of war

Churchill was accused of not having formulated the declaration of war he had sent Japan harshly enough. He replied: "If I want to kill somebody, why shouldn't I tell them politely?"

Clarification

Houston had told me so many new things about events of which my knowledge had been very superficial. But I needed more details on one of his statements. "You are talking about the Japanese wanting to enforce peace negotiations. I don't understand. The war had only started after their attack on Pearl Harbor."

Uninformed

You are just as uninformed as the American population was back then when Japan's "surprise attack" hit them. There was a certain vague suspicion that secret powerful US elites were planning a war against Japan. But nobody knew any details about that. The initiative "America first" preached: First, improve our country's infrastructure, boost our economy, ameliorate the living conditions of the working class. We don't need a war against Japan.

Roosevelt could only laugh at that. These idiots don't even know that we have been at war with Japan for five years already.

Chinese-Japanese war

With vast amounts of money, the American leaders had managed to turn the generalissimo Chiang Kai-shek against the Communist International, the Comintern, and into a nationalist. In order to prove his role as the new leader of China, this giant country, he was supposed to conquer Korea. Which, back then, belonged to Japan. The USA provided Chiang Kai-shek with all the money and arms he needed. In addition, the American Secret Service assisted him by provoking incidents that lead to shootouts, since that is still crucial for starting a war, at least in the hot phase.

Modern writers

Houston paused for a bit. Then he laughed and said: "It's marvelous how much modern technology makes all our lives easier. In earlier times, a writer would have needed to present and describe all of these incidents." I, however, can say: "If you're interested, you can find the details on the internet." Long live the Internet and Wikipedia.

The course of the war

The war between China and Japan didn't go as Roosevelt had imagined. Instead of a quick conquest of Korea, they suffered harsh setbacks. Roosevelt threatened to pull Chiang Kai-shek's funds, to which Chiang replied by threatening to cease all military operations. Of course, that would have been the worst case scenario.

Flying tigers

Roosevelt had no choice but to actively step up and help the Chinese. He placed his elite air force, the flying tigers, at their disposal. The Internet has pictures of their boldly painted planes. Officially, they couldn't be there on government orders, which is why they were presented as volunteers. Roosevelt even stated that they were rebellious pilots who had deserted their posts against the government's express wishes. However, he was still the one paying their salaries and if they lost a plane, it was replaced using American army supplies.

Utmost secrecy

The fact that a five-year war and a fighter group as big as the flying tigers had been hidden from an entire nation for several years seems almost impossible. Well, if the press plays along, then where are people supposed to get that information? Even FDR's predecessor, President Herbert Hoover, had no idea about this secret war with Japan. He was as utterly surprised by the attack on Pearl Harbor as everybody else.
That attack seemed to come out of nowhere. Only Roosevelt and Churchill knew the truth.

Museum (3.6)

Armenian Cognac

A small museum is connected to the part of the war rooms that holds the living quarters. There are many displays on boards. A huge table catches the eye. On it are everyday items of Churchill's life, for example, empty bottles of champagne. Next to them are bills for wine deliveries. Churchill's considerable need for whisky was met by his friend Johnny Walker, who gave it to him as a present. Word of his love of Armenian Cognac got out and led to Stalin using state funds to commission a yearly gift shipment of a box of Cognac ever since the Yalta Conference.

More beautiful than any love letter

In Churchill's opinion, that Cognac was better than the most exquisite Fines de Champagne. It was so high-proof that Churchill began to experience serious problems, making his family suffer as well. His hands started to shake so badly that he wasn't able to hold a glass anymore. He himself had to acknowledge that he couldn't carry on this way. A withdrawal treatment seemed unavoidable and it was successful. He told his beloved Clementine about it. He wrote: Once again, my hands are sure, the shaking has gone. During the last three days, I was once again able to shoot 144 songbirds. Clementine's answer shows her great joy. Her letter is displayed in the museum. "Your letter has made me happier than the most beautiful love letter could have."

Armenian rebellion

Churchill got his first taste of this Cognac because he was spending some time in Armenia. England had installed and equipped several cells that were secretly working against the sultan. They were paid by the English government. Today, Putin would classify them as agents because of this. They were trying to prepare a planned war against the Ottoman Empire by weakening the government. To this end, the British were seeking the assistance of the Armenian church, which was supposed to ideologically support the rebellion against the Muslim sultan. They also trained snipers and gave them logistical aid. More than ten senior government officials were murdered with English help. Even an attempt on the sultan's life can be traced back to an English initiative.

Genocide

When the war had started and the Armenians were rebelling, the Istanbul government didn't know how to help themselves. Furthermore, they were fearing a collaboration between the revolutionaries and the Russian Armenians. The only solution they could think of was to relocate the Armenians. By now, we all know the catastrophic consequences of this forced relocation. However, the English incitement is generally kept secret.

It's understandable that Erdogan refuses to let the Turkish take all the blame for this disaster.

Empty champagne bottles

These bottles are a reminder of Churchill's close friendship with Jinnah, who had left India and lived in London for many years. He was Muslim and not supposed to drink alcohol. But since he advocated a secularized Islam, the alcohol ban didn't apply to him. Churchill saw him as an ally against Mahatma Gandhi, who was threatening England's domination over India. Jinnah liked living in England so much that he had stopped even thinking about returning until Churchill urged him to finally take up the fight against Gandhi. And so Jinnah was sent back to India with 100 trained fighters and 100 million dollars.

The founder of a state

Each of these 100 fighters was supposed to in turn train 100 other fighters. The 100 million dollars were to be used for this. Afterwards, the fight was to be taken to Gandhi. Jinnah actually managed to separate Muslims and Hindus. This led to 1 million casualties and 13 million expellees, but also to the foundation of two states, India and Pakistan (at first, Pakistan was still divided up into East and West Pakistan). Jinnah is seen as the founder of the Pakistani state. His impressive mausoleum can be admired in Karachi.

Gandhi's assassination

During their goodbye, Churchill had advised his friend: "Choose a Hindu to assassinate Gandhi. It absolutely should not be a Muslim, people would suspect it was your doing right away." So that's how it was done and Churchill was immensely satisfied to live to see Gandhi assassinated in 1947. The champagne binges had paid off.

In WWII, Jinnah provided England with soldiers. However, he himself died only a year after Gandhi's assassination. Today, Pakistan is no longer really an ally to England and the USA. In the end, Churchill's plan didn't work out.
What's left today is the animosity between India and Pakistan, Hindus and Muslims. For centuries, they had lived side by side peacefully.

Caricatures (3.7)

Pit bull and tiger

The museum has very nice caricatures that show Churchill as a pit bull and his friend Clemenceau as a tiger. These two shared a life-long friendship and were both very proud that people called them bullenbeisser and cat of prey.

Weekend

Clemenceau used to fly up from Paris for the weekend and spend it with his friend Churchill in his private house in Chartwell. During their drinking bouts, they imagined how they would divide the German colonies in Africa – at a time when the war hadn't even broken out yet.

Churchill wanted German East Africa so that no enclave would be left between English colonies from Cairo to Cape Town. Clemenceau wanted Cameroon and Ghana so that the French colonial territory in West Africa would be connected.

Baghdad and Damascus

Since both were sure that they would be able to pull the Ottoman Empire into the war once it had finally broken out, they also started dividing the rest of the Ottoman Empire, seeing as England had already conquered Egypt and France had snatched Algeria and Tunesia.

Churchill annexed the fruitful land of Mesopotamia, today known as Iraq, in the name of England, including of course its legendary capital Baghdad. He was greatly angered that the German emperor had built the Baghdad railway up to it.

For France, Clemenceau claimed the magnificent city of Damascus, where the German emperor had made his famous toast to Muslims, much to Clemenceau's outrage. Along with that, he wanted the surrounding land of Syria.

Mossul

While making the borders, they had to make sure that the rich oil fields around Mossul still fell to England. That is why they cut the Kurdish settlement area in two with an artificial border, which since then has been causing high tensions and confrontations unto this day.

Jerusalem

Obviously, Churchill claimed the Holy Land, Palestine, for himself, the land where his friend Baruch wanted to establish a Jewish state according to Herzel's model. And these fantasies, conjured up during a wine binge, actually came true later. The Balfour Declaration that was ordered by Churchill promised the Americans that the Jews would be allowed to found their state in Palestine, causing them to enter the World War. Only three days later, the first battleships landed on the Palestinian shore to conquer the land. Balfour had promised it to the Jews before the English had even conquered it.

Lebanon

Since England got the much sought-after country of Palestine, Lebanon and Beyrouth had to be conceded to France.
As you can see, these drinking binges in Chartwell weren't just pointless bouts of alcoholism – world history was written here.

Betrayal

In their fantasies, Pit bull and Tiger ruthlessly betrayed one of their most important allies: the Arab King Feysal. The great and exceptionally gifted archeologist Lawrence of Arabia had gained the monarch's trust. The foundation of his power was his possession of the Holy Cities Mecca and Medina. Lawrence was supposed to get him to orchestrate an Arab rebellion against the sultan of Istanbul. As a reward, he was promised he would become the leader of a united Arab Empire, the most important centers of which would be Damascus, Baghdad, Beyrouth, Jerusalem, Amman, and, to the south of Mecca, all of Yemen. Churchill gave Lawrence plenty of rope, leaving almost limitless funds at his disposal. As long as the battle lasted, Feysal demanded 350,000 pounds a month. It lasted more than 2 years. And Churchill and Clemenceau weren't done with their back-stabbing. Since they feared that Feysal would fight back once he noticed that he'd been had, they instigated Ibn Saud to attack Feysal's heartland, the fortified city of Rijad, and also Mecca and Medina while Feysal's troops were tied up fighting the sultan in the north. Lawrence of Arabia certainly wasn't in on their betrayal.

Porky Pig

Another charming caricature, this time drawn by Churchill himself, can be seen in the museum. He drew himself as a pig, which was his wife Clementine's loving nickname for him. He was delighted by that nickname. He thought that pigs had so many human traits. Dogs are too servile, cats too malicious. But pigs are so delightfully similar to us humans.

Painting (3.8)

Talent

Churchill was actually a talented painter. A slide show presents all of his paintings. They mostly show landscapes in the South of France. He preferred painting trees, especially pines. "Trees don't bitch if I don't get the picture in their likeness, people however..."

Portraits

He nonetheless experimented with painting portraits, trying to realistically copy photographs. He became quite proficient, which even earned him the title Master of Arts by the Royal Academy of Arts.

Therapy

Oftentimes, painting was his therapy when depression came to haunt him. He himself has said that the first thing he would do in the afterlife would be to paint 10 million pictures so he could recuperate from the stress of life. "It's all so boring" is how he summarized his life at the end of his days.

Comparison

As we know, Hitler also liked to paint and, astonishingly enough, the two of them had a similar style. Their color shading is almost identical and their style could be called post-impressionist. However, architectonic structures usually predominate in Hitler's paintings. Churchill was particularly happy when he got the advantage over his rival in direct comparison. For example, one of his paintings earned him 60,000 pounds while the highest price for a Hitler painting was only 40,000 pounds.

Witticisms (3.9)

Collection

Churchill's witticisms are famous. Collections of his bon mots are online. They are so well-known that almost everyone can quote them. For example: „The only statistics you can trust are those you falsified yourself" or "Contracts are made to be broken."

If two people share the same opinion, then one of them is dispensable.

If a smoker reads about the dangers of smoking, he will likely stop – reading.

The main defect of democracy are the elections.

It pays to make mistakes that you can learn from early on.

You can always count on Americans to do the right thing – after they've tried everything else.

His response to being invited to the Armageddon Party at the Savoy is also quite funny: "Of course I will come. I wouldn't miss the end of the world for anything. However, I'll have to go to the dentist first, I don't want to see the end with a tooth gap."

Armageddon happens about 2-3 times almost every year. In 1946, it actually was a global phenomenon.

Teeth

Churchill's teeth were very bad and he was forced to wear braces early on. Several teeth were missing and the rest were connected with golden wires. If his valet forgot to lay out his dentures, he occasionally went to Parliament without them. The thought of a picture of him with gaps in his teeth filled him with fear. That would be a catastrophe. Almost as bad as a paparazzi managing to take a picture of the Queen picking her nose. In these situations, he didn't dare to open his mouth. He didn't smile, he didn't greet people, he just sat there with clenched teeth and a fierce expression. He would always apologize and explain later.

Speech defect

As a child, Churchill stuttered. He did manage to overcome this problem, except for one little speech defect. He wasn't able to pronounce the s, it always came out as sh. Typically for him, he thought that this was what made his speeches charming. Whenever a dentist had to make him new dentures, they were reminded to make them in a way that would preserve this defect.

During big state events, if he was standing close to the Queen, he would always sing into her ear with great enthusiasm, "God shave the Queen."
He resented the Queen for having married a German and this was his small form of revenge.

Prince Philip

Philip was the bone of contention. Churchill accused the young Queen: "the English people have sacrificed so much to destroy the Germans. And you, their future Queen, go and marry a German. It's bad enough that German blood is running in your veins as well, but you just can't ask the nation to suffer this marriage."

Prince Philip, who was present during their exchange, wanted to calm him down and said: "Dear Uncle Churchill, why don't you just call me the Viking? That's what Frankyboy does," meaning the American Franklin Roosevelt. "But your names give away your German heritage. Your mother is a Princess of Battenberg and through her, you are even in line to the Greek throne."

"Then we'll just change her name to Mount Batten; that is what my uncle, the viceroy of India, did."

"But how will we translate your father's name? It's Holstein-Sonderburg-Glücksburg."

"Ah, we'll be broadminded and translate it with Windsor. That's what the Sachsen-Coburg-Gotha are called."

"And through that, you are an heir to the Danish throne. If you should take that throne, people will say: the king of this tiny country is married to the Queen of England and the Indian Empress."

"I will waive my claim to the Danish throne."

"It is simply out of the question that Elisabeth marries a German and that's my final word!"

Now Elisabeth got involved.

"You toothless grandpa, you can say whatever you want, but I'll marry him anyway."

"Then you can count on something: until the day I die, I will make sure that he gets nothing but bad press."

Elisabeth's reply: "You can kiss my… and stick that where…"

Doubt

At that point, I just had to interrupt Houston. Now you're exaggerating again. I find it entirely impossible that these royal lips could have ever uttered a sentence like "kiss my... and stick that where..."

Blessed marriage

Just a few days ago, Elisabeth and her beloved Philip were able to celebrate their 70th anniversary.

None of her three kids were that lucky. All three have been divorced. A particularly tragic divorce was that of Charles and Diana.

Gibraltar

While talking about teeth, Houston remembered another story that Churchill himself had told once in a club. Hitler and Mussolini met with Franco in Hendaye, on the French-Spanish border. The Second World War had just started and Hitler was suggesting he could conquer Gibraltar, which was currently occupied by the English, and give it back to Spain after the war. Gibraltar was important for blocking access to the Mediterranean at this strait. Quite the reasonable suggestion, actually. However, what Hitler didn't know was that the English had gotten wind of his plan. Since Franco got the money to pay his army and his generals from Rothschild, just like his opponents, the Communist International, did, his generals were offered 2 million dollars each if they refused to agree to this plan.

Difficult negotiations

Since Franco could hardly admit that his generals were refusing to obey him, the negotiations were fruitless. However, they were so difficult that Hitler later said that he would rather have his teeth pulled out one by one than negotiate with Franco again.

Final photograph

The newspapers printed a final photograph of the three negotiators Hitler, Franco, and Mussolini. It shows that the negotiations had also afflicted Franco a lot. His expression on the picture was so desperate that the journalist didn't dare to publish it like that. He pasted another picture of Franco over his crestfallen face. However, he did such a bad job of it that even the printers all noticed it. It lead to wild laughter. The photograph with the paste-job can be accessed through the archives.

Authentic?

Churchill relished the fact that his witticisms met with such approval. Some phrases were circulating that he hadn't coined himself, but he liked them anyway and he adopted them. In the mornings, he often asked his servant: "Did I say something funny yesterday?" and the latter would always faithfully tell him what people were attributing to him.

At the Pearly Gates

This remark surely isn't authentic. He supposedly said it to Saint Peter in order to be let into Heaven. The saint asked him if he had ever done any good deed in his life, not just wage wars and throw bombs.

"Certainly. I have helped millions of young women in many countries get their widow's pension very early." Saint Peter wasn't quite sure if all of these women were happy about that. That is why he first wanted to ask the Central Council of Archangels whether this would count as a good deed.

"Have you done any good deed for men?" "Of course. At no cost to them, I made sure they got prosthetic limbs and glass eyes."

"Well, the fact that they didn't have to pay for it is surely a good thing," Saint Peter said. And so he at least let dear Churchill into Purgatory.

Dear God

Churchill was an atheist. When asked if he believed in God, he replied: „He hasn't introduced himself to me yet. But should we actually meet and should he ask for my list of sins, he will probably die of shock when he hears how many skeletons are in my closet." "And how about Satan, do you believe in him?" "I don't have to believe in him; him I meet daily."

Life line (3.10)

90 times 365

There's a 15-meter round installation with Churchill's "life line" in the museum. It is a touchscreen and leads directly to a digital file cabinet containing every note on Churchill that's available on every individual day. There is not a single day without at least a few notes. It's the most detailed life story any person has. Notes are available for each day, from the day he was born to the day he died. There's not even enough time to go through all of them; that would take months.
I just want to pick out a few incidents.

Houston told me that at home, he already had a written record called "Churchill's tales." Those are stories Churchill himself told while spending his evenings in the club. Houston said he would give me this collection to read soon.

Journalist

Some of these stories were also written down by Churchill himself in the records he kept as a journalist on his many travels. On his drive from Cairo to Cape Town, he had the opportunity to participate in the Battle of Omdurman. His printed work is called 'river war' and recounts the rebellion against the English colonial power at the upper Nile.

The last cavalry battle

60,000 equestrians and camel-riders stood to defy the attacking Englishmen. They wanted to keep their independence, which their great Mahdi had won for them, at any cost. But they were trying to defend it with sabers and their bravery didn't help them against the modern fire arms of the British. They were all massacred, along with their horses and camels. Churchill writes about it: "there could hardly be anyone less welcome than we were."

Mausoleum

The mausoleum of their great liberation fighter Mahdi had become a pilgrimage site. He was worshiped like a saint. The belligerent General Kitchener had his body exhumed. The bones were ground up and spread across the Nile. The skull was used as an ash tray during the victory celebrations and Churchill also tapped the ash off his cigar on it.

Protest

Their actions sparked a strong protest, not only amongst the population of this country, but amongst the entire world public. Churchill himself had to admit that it was ill-advised to hurt the natives' feelings this way. Besides, it didn't give the victors any kind of advantage.

Funeral

That is why the English government gave orders that at least the remaining skull be buried once again. The "ash tray" was interred following a ceremonious procession of the entire population.

Boer War (3.11)

Cape Town

Was the end point of the traverse of Africa. That is where Cecil Rhodes was to be found, who, just a few months earlier, had conquered Southern and Northern Rhodesia. Today, these countries are called Zimbabwe and Mozambique. Nothing is supposed to be reminiscent of the hated conqueror Rhodes. He had learned that lots of gold and diamonds had been found in South Africa. He wanted to add the yields of those mines to his already vast stolen wealth.

Boers

The problem with this plan was that the Boers had settled in South Africa. Boer is the Dutch word for farmer. The Dutch didn't see South Africa as a colony, they saw it as a settlement area that they wanted to till themselves. Comparable to the Pilgrim Fathers in North American states. The Boers didn't want some foreigner to come and exploit their gold mines.

Discrimination

The English saw that as ethnic discrimination and accused the Boers of violating Rhodes' human rights. An English army was sent to South Africa to establish humane conditions there. The truth, that the actual goal of this operation was to have the mines exploited under English management, was studiously kept secret.

450,000 soldiers

Is what Queen Victoria sent to break down the Boers' resistance. The Crown was to get 20% of all profits. The Boer War was new to the English as they were now fighting civilized Europeans as opposed to the Negros, who were seen as inferior and uncivilized.

Guerrillas

Only 30,000 Boers faced this giant army. Of course, they would never have been able to win in a regular land battle. They therefore hid during the day, attacked at night time, and sabotaged the railways. This made the English situation hopeless.

Concentration camps

It all changed when Cecil Rhodes had the idea to gather their women and children in concentration camps. They were held without food or water and after 3-4 weeks, all of them had died. That's when the resistance of the guerilla fighters began to crumble. With their women and children dead, they saw no point in continuing the fight.

A new tactic

In this, Churchill found a new tactic he could use in his later wars. "It's more important to kill women and children since that's how the men's morale is destroyed." He employed this tactic when ordering the bombing of German cities. The men were fighting at the frontlines; pretty much the only people living in the cities were women, children, and maybe care-dependent old parents.

This offered a perfect opportunity to undermine the men's morale. That is why Churchill called these bomb attacks "morale bombing."

The importance of women (3.12)

Another big advantage of this tactic is that it is much more effective to kill the women if one wants to obliterate a people. A simple example illustrates this point: If 1,000 women and 3-4 men survive, the birth rate amounts to 1,000, no matter what. That's higher than in the reverse situation: If 1,000 men and 3 women survive, the men can try whatever they want, but still there won't be more than 3 children. In ten years, it would be 30.

This example shows how expendable men are. Churchill, befitting to his English humor, hoped that this appreciation of women would lead to him becoming the eternal honorary chairman of all women's communities.

Experiment

In search of scientific proof for this theory, an experiment was conducted with female and male rats. The experiment confirmed the theory.
However, there are serious scientists who doubt the validity of this experiment. The sexual behavior of rats is not necessarily comparable to that of humans. Repeating the experiment with human subjects will hardly be easily feasible. It would take at least 10 years and it's doubtful whether enough test subjects would volunteer to participate in the experiment.

Vénus hottentotte

And yet, Mother Nature herself has given us proof that the survival of women is more important to her than the survival of men. The Hottentotten live in the Kalahari Desert, which is so hostile to life that the people there often go months without finding food. A genetic mutation has occurred there, however, it only affects women. They can survive up to six months without food. Nature has given them Steatopygia, a very adipose backside which provides them with fat that they can live off. It's comparable to the humps of a camel or a dromedary, which serve the same purpose. The hump limply hangs down once the fat reserve is depleted.

Sarah Baartman

This "vénus hottentotte" has become famous. For money, she would show off her adipose backside. The Parisian Musée de l'homme has a life-size plaster statue of her. The English brought the living Baartman into their country and people in London also got to admire this miracle of nature.

Future plans

After all of Africa had been conquered, English imperialism suddenly stood without goal. But Churchill had an idea: they hadn't yet taken all of the Ottoman Sultan's territories. The Middle East was still open for conquest. The fruitful land of Mesopotamia was, in Churchill's opinion, far too valuable to be inhabited by uncivilized tribes. Only the highly civilized English would be apt to take possession of such a colony. In addition, people had already started to convert their ship motors from coal to oil. That's why the rich oil fields of Basra also had to be acquired by the English.

One of the most skilled archeologists, Lawrence of Arabia, was chosen to prepare this conquest. Houston says: "I will tell you this story in detail some other time."

Blow up (3.13)

We opened the archive to read about a smaller story. The blow up in Sydney Street. Back then, Churchill was minister of the interior and his ministry wasn't far from Sydney Street. When he heard shots fired, he ran immediately to the location where they had been fired. During shootouts, Churchill couldn't be stopped, he just had to participate.

Mauser pistol

For his 18th birthday, Churchill's mother had given him a Mauser pistol. A very sensible present for a young man. It would be nice if that custom were adopted by German mothers. Churchill always carried the pistol with him his whole life. He had attached so many memories of enemies slain with this pistol that he didn't want to exchange it even when an improved version came onto the market.

The original model has since become an iconic weapon and can be bought at various weapons factories. It costs between 99 and 300 dollars.

Sydney Street

Two burglars had entered a jewelry store there with pistols drawn. When the house was surrounded by police, they started shooting at people in the street. Churchill shot back and the two bandits finally realized they had no chance of escaping. That's why they started a fire, hoping that the chaos of ambulances and firefighters would give them a chance to escape after all. Churchill, in his role as Interior Minister, forbade the fire department from putting out the fire and so they let the house burn to the ground. When people later entered the ruins of the house, they found the two thugs sitting in the lowest basement level, huddled together and burnt to a cinder.

Fire rider

Maybe some of you know the German fire rider poem by Mörike. This burnt fire rider sits on his horse, leaning against the wall, until someone touches him. Then the ashes fall down. The same fate awaited the two bandits when Churchill gave orders to have them transported to the chamber of horrors as a warning example: don't set fire to a house that you're sitting in. But when people tried to pick them up, their bodies were reduced to a pile of ash. They had no choice but to sweep up the bandits with brooms.

Criticism

Churchill's role in this situation has been severely criticized, seeing as he was Interior Minister at the time.
For one, you don't just start firing shots like that and second, a fire has to be extinguished. You can't let anyone burn to death, not even bandits.
Churchill replied that all this was just defamation and that he had not even been present during the robbery.
But since photo cameras had already been invented back then and one picture published in a newspaper clearly shows Churchill in the front line, he had to retract his statement. He

said: "Well, obviously an Interior Minister has to be fighting in the front lines when such crimes are being committed."

All-clear

At first, a terrorist background had been suspected, but soon authorities could give their all-clear. The two thieves had been entirely normal thugs. All this excitement for nothing.

Minister of finance (3.13)

Booming economy

In 1926, the English economy was doing so well that entrepreneurs were bringing in huge profits. They had so much equity capital that they no longer needed to borrow money in order to pay for resources and workers. Usually, the banks needed to pay that money up front and only got it back once the product was finalized. This new development brought the banks great displeasure since they were living off loan interests. So they needed a minister of finance to ruin the economy so that banks would be needed once again.

Change of parties

It was hard to find a respectable person to do this job. For Churchill, this wasn't an issue. His only problem was that the Conservative Party formed the government at the time and, after all, he had previously switched sides and joined the Labour Party. But this was an easy problem to solve – Churchill simply rejoined the Conservatives. His comment: "It takes a strong character to change parties once, but to do it twice, one has to be a leader as I am."

Deflation

What followed shows how easy it is for politicians to ruin the economy. It only took Churchill half a year. He returned to the gold standard. Most banks simply couldn't give out money anymore and companies with lots of contracts couldn't fulfill them anymore and neither could they pay their workers. Their companies could often be bought by the banks at the symbolic prize of one pound. However, getting the companies up and running again, that wasn't quite as easy. Neither banks nor politicians are able to do that and the entrepreneurs were sick and tired of being treated this way.

General strike

It went so far that a general strike was called that turned the country's situation into a fiasco. Even Churchill was at his wits' end, the only solution he could think of was to shoot the strikers down, following Napoleon's principle: "if twelve people die, it's a catastrophe; if 10,000 are killed, peace can finally return."

Fortunately, his suggestion was never put into action. He overcame this crisis like many others – with a good aphorism. "Some say that I'm the worst minister of finance England has ever had. I have to admit, it's true."

In the desert

Churchill had caused this economic depression as ordered, meaning the banks were now satisfied; still, the English government didn't dare to give him another public position from then on. He calls this his years in the desert. That isn't quite true. He was still the grey-haired eminence because he represented the world of high finance.

Wallstreet

His reputation reached Wallstreet in New York. When Herbert Hoover, whom the banks hated, was elected president in 1928, they invited Churchill to New York. He was supposed to help them cause a great depression so that the elected president Hoover would be ruined in the eyes of the public. His promise of general wealth would then be seen as unrealistic.

Black Thursday

This plan met with success within a quarter of a year. All bank owners got together and discussed how they could best manage to pull off a bank crash. When asked what the hell he was doing there, Churchill answered: "I just wanted to relax a little in New York." The banks' approach was this: They decided amongst themselves which banks would go bankrupt and which banks would store the good money. If a bank goes bankrupt, that only means that depositors lose their savings and securities. The bank itself bears no consequences. Banks are only involved with 5%. And so the gold reserves were transported to the private basements of Rockefeller and Rothschild by the tons and the money was transferred to a bank only insiders knew about. To make the whole thing legal, the banks that had transferred their money received security papers for the same amount. However, these papers were completely worthless. One could call them highrisk papers or, more truthfully, fantasy obligations artificially created to deceive the public.

Baruch

Him we already know. From WWI to WWII, he was the actual secret president of the USA. He was often asked to offer himself as a presidential candidate, but he said: "Why should I? I lead the country without having to face the public. I don't have to stand for re-election and no one can criticize me." He played a crucial role in the bank crisis. Naturally, he not only saved his assets and those of his friend Churchill but multiplied them. While the vast majority had lost everything, it was easy for those not concerned by the crisis to acquire companies, houses, etc. inexpensively. For example, George Untermeier, who had wanted to buy the Washington Post for 5 million dollars and couldn't get it at that price, was able to purchase the newspaper for a mere 800,000 dollars during a foreclosure. Kennedy, father to the President Kennedy we all know, was one of the insiders. His estate was valued at about 2 million before the Great Depression; two years later, it was valued at 100 million. Others show a similar increase.

Autobiography

Churchill writes: "I was taking a walk along Wallstreet and was surprised by all the excitement. One guy was jumping out a window, another was yelling like a madman. A journalist wanted to sell his car for 100 dollars because the banks weren't able to give out money anymore." Churchill pretended to be astounded by it when in actual fact, he was quite gleeful that the bank crash had worked out so successfully.

Black Friday

In New York, this crash occured on Thursday. The European banks didn't crash until the following day. Churchill wanted to see how his fellow countrymen in London would react. He quickly boarded a plane and flew back and was very proud of his English people. Very unlike the Americans who had been howling in protest, the Londoners politely retreated to the back rooms of their houses and shot themselves. They really kept the proverbial stiff upper lip.

Woodrow Wilson

Houston had so much more to tell me. Especially about his encounter with Wilson in 1918. He's the president who had declared war on Germany in 1916. He also signed the document for the foundation of the FED (Federal Reserve Bank). As the son of a Methodist preacher, he was also very interested in the Westminster Central Hall, the impressive center of this religious community, which can be seen from the Treasury.

Franklin Delano Roosevelt

Houston also wanted to tell me some more stories about him. It was obvious however that the life story of this great statesman who had dominated world history for almost 100 years couldn't be reviewed with just one visit to the war rooms.

French House (3.14)

We were pretty tired and decided to spend a relaxed evening in the French House. Their French cuisine is exquisite. However, we opted for a rather simple meal without meat, a vegetable stew with wonderfully fresh vegetables the French call Ratatouille. To complement our meal, we drank Chablis, a light white wine. You cannot leave French House without drinking a Ricardo Permod first, a delightful anise liqueur. The atmosphere is still reminiscent of the fact that General De Gaulle was living here during the war. He even wrote his famous TV speech "We are not alone" here.

Georges Brassens

Music was very discreetly playing in the background, songs by this great chansonnier. He, like no other, has shaped the attitude towards life of the post-war generation and was an outstanding favorite of Parisian students most of all. Everybody was so fed up with war and march music. As we walked to the door, the sounds of "la musique qui au pas cela ne me regarde pas" were still in our ears.

Diary

On our way to the subway, I confessed to my friend Houston that I had written down all of his stories in the form of a diary. Today had been our third day. We agreed that on the next day, we would meet in front of the Art Gallery and afterwards even visit the British Museum.

Invitation

Houston revealed that he had gotten an invitation from Cynthia and Charles via email. They were inviting us to their house on Eaton Square. Douglas would be there as well and as our theme for the evening, Cynthia had chosen "la guerra parallela." The corresponding stories would tell of something they had experienced during a vacation, comparable to the one in Nice. This time, they had been in Naples and were currently south of the city in the bay of Paestum when they met the son of a high-ranking Black Shirt.

Antonio

This son, Antonio, had later relocated to London and was running a very popular Italian restaurant. If you cross London Bridge and keep on straight ahead, you'll walk right towards it; it's called Padella. He does not offer traiteur service. However, he makes an exception for us since he belongs to the circle of friends. We're having pasta alle vongole as a first course. After that, Saltimbocca and delightfully fresh green salads of various kinds with exquisite olive oil and wine vinegar, served with Chianti. As a dessert, we get freshly whipped Zabaione as only Italians know how to make. Antonio doesn't attach value to intricate ornaments, to him it's just important that the food tastes good. He is a gourmet sans chic, meaning his food is intended for connoisseurs who can do without all the foofaraw.

The 4th Day (4)

Art Gallery (4.1)

I got there early and walked up the impressive staircase to the entrance. A huge Perspex money box is standing there. It was filled to about a quarter with coins, but also with small and big banknotes. English museums are free and visitors can put a contribution in the box if they want. Houston wasn't there yet and I had a chance to calmly examine the panoramic view of this marvelous city. At the right, I could see the oversized pillar with Admiral Nelson on it and four gigantic lions at its base. Straight ahead, I had a view of Whitehall Street, with nothing but palaces on both sides. Another great view is that of Big Ben and Parliament House. A small side street on the right leads to 10 Downing Street, which is however closed off to the public. From here, it becomes obvious that London is not only the capital of an important country, but also of the biggest world empire of all time.

Dame Myra

Soon, I saw Houston climbing the steps. The first thing I asked him was: "Where did Dame Myra's piano stand?" This gifted pianist was a London favorite. At the beginning of the war, the German air raids started and the Londoners had to flee to the shelters – in this case, into the subway stations because London wasn't prepared for air attacks. Because of this, nobody dared give concerts anymore since the short interval between the alarm and the actual attack left no time to evacuate big concert halls. Dame Myra had the idea to simply relocate concerts to public places. Since it was impossible to charge people there, these concerts were free.

Robert Schumann

Many of her colleagues followed suit and her idea was applauded. For her, these concerts were serving two purposes. She wanted to oppose Churchill's rants about Germany, who only referred to the Germans by calling them the Huns. Myra wanted to present another side of Germany. She played music by Schumann, who is seen as the epitome of German Romanticism. Therefore, her concerts were a quiet protest against official politics and the Londoners were enraptured by her performance of Schumann's Reverie, Carnaval, Papillo, and Aufschwung (upswing).

Comparison

Churchill was appalled and wanted to shoot her right there on her piano stool. However, he didn't dare do it because Dame Myra was Jewish and even Churchill couldn't risk being seen as an anti-semite. He pointed out that he was well aware that the pianist was using her music as a form of protest against his anti-German rhetoric, but that – unlike Hitler's Germany – his government guaranteed artistic freedom.

Marquis of Posa

Quite the opposite to what had happened in the Schiller Theater in Berlin. During a performance of "Don Carlos," the Marquis of Posa urges the king: "Sire, grant freedom of thought." At this, the audience had gotten up and applauded. At once, the SS had marched in and the audience had quickly settled down again and stopped applauding.

Courage

If you consider the situation, air raids on London, you have to admit that the pianist showed a lot of courage by playing music by a German Romanticist.

Wochenschau

At the same time, the German news program, Wochenschau, was showing pictures of the bombs that were meant for London. The biggest bomb was titled "an extra thick cigar for Churchill."

Painting

We entered the museum. Even the architectural design of the entrance hall is already superb. The collection of paintings is so overwhelming that you don't know which painting to talk about first. The Grotto Madonna by Leonardo da Vinci, the breathtaking paintings by Turner, by Constable, and so on and so forth.

The Ambassadors

I just have to mention one darling scene. A small group of first-graders and their teacher came to look at Hans Holbein the Younger's "The Ambassadors." We stayed with them for the whole lesson and listened.

The lesson

The children, both boys and girls, sat down on the floor in front of the painting and the teacher started to ask them some questions. "Now, take a look at the two men – what are they wearing?" The tiny hands shot up and the kids told her how they perceived the men's clothes. "What's that on their heads? Now look at their shoes. What's that lying on the floor? What can you see on the table and on that small bench in front of it? Do you notice something special about their belts? What can you tell me about their hands?" The small group was so interested and disciplined, it surprised me. After this, the teacher handed out pieces of paper and crayons to each pupil and asked them to draw just one single detail. Each kid picked a different detail, one drew a ring on a finger, another the buckle on a shoe, an item on the table...

At the end, the teacher collected their drawings and said "now we go back to school, look at each one of your drawings, and talk about them." With this, the children quietly cleared out.

Envy

How privileged those kids are to be introduced to culture so soon and to learn about their country's history at that young age. The teacher did choose not to reveal the secret of the dead man's skull that is hidden within the painting. Her pupils were still way too young to hear about that.

Holbein

Holbein is one of the greatest painters. He was born in Basel, where he already painted Erasmus of Rotterdam and Thomas

Morus, the author of "Utopia." Later, he went to London. He painted all the famous pictures linked to Henry VIII, pictures of Anne Boleyn and Jane Seymour, the king's third wife, who had given birth to his only son but died doing so.

Holbein also died in London, sadly at a pretty young age. The English see him as one of their own, just like Händel.

German paintings

It came as a big surprise to me that in all this abundance of paintings from all over the world, not one painting by a German artist was exhibited. This is a result of English politics, whose official representatives believe that, "There is no Germany, never has been and never will be."

Dürer

The only exception is a self-portrait of Dürer. It was stolen from the protestant city Nuremberg during the Thirty Years' War and brought to Vienna by catholic troops. From there, it travelled to Madrid, where it was seized by Louis XIV and taken to Paris. There, the English took possession of it and it finally ended up in London. Maybe Hermann Goering isn't the only art thief out there.

Break

We took a small break and went to the comfortable café, which is attached to the gallery, for a small drink. A visit to the museum is in fact quite exhausting. There, Houston told me that in the evening, we were invited to Cynthia and Charles's home on Eaton Square. We were supposed to come a little early since there would be dinner.

Exit

On our way out, we looked at paintings by Rembrandt, Frans Hals, Jan von Eyck. Then we crossed Trafalgar Square so we could eat lunch in Jamie Oliver's Fifteen.

Lunch (4.2)

Houston suggested we try one of Jamie's famous fish soups. England, a country surrounded by the ocean, truly has no shortage of fish. I was pleased by his suggestion, seeing as one of my favorite dishes is French bouillabaisse. Now I would finally get to try the English version.

Diary

While we were waiting, I revealed to Houston that I had been writing down everything he, and also the others during our evening at his place, had told me in form of a diary. Also, that I wanted to publish it since I thought it was very interesting.

Title

However, I wasn't quite sure about the title yet. "London diary" is too generic. "Strange stories from London?" Well, some of the stories are actually pretty normal. "Incredible London stories" also doesn't apply to all of them. "Alternative Short Stories" would hint at the fact that not all of them are politically correct. And that would be too political.

The London Decameron

Another title I am considering. It's neutral and only refers to its formal division. As we all know, ten young aristocrats, seven men and three women, were fleeing from Florence in fear of the Plague. They chose to settle down in a country house outside the city limits. To pass the time, each one of them was to think up a story to then tell the others. And that day after day. This way, within 10 days, they had ten stories for each day, giving them 100 stories in total.

Boccaccio

He is the author. He was a priest and in confession he heard many a scandalous tale about adultery, robbery, and murder. In my London version, this doesn't come into play, but some of your stories are also quite scandalous.

The fourth day

Today is our fourth day. We do only have four storytellers and not ten. And not everyone has the same number of stories to tell. You, Tusitala, are the main storyteller. My role is that of documentation. But since I am free to add comments, voice criticism, and to even tell stories of my own, I could be counted as a fifth participant. This way, we have at least half of the aristocratic party of Florence. And maybe we'll even pull off ten days, too.

Fish soup

By the way, the fish soup was excellent. And the famous TV cook is also really likeable.

British Museum (4.3)

The giant glass ceiling over the courtyard is overwhelming. It is the biggest roofed space in Europe. In the middle of the yard, you can find the domed building of the reading room. To the right and left are the entrance doors to the Egyptian section and to the Greek collections. From the gallery, you have the most beautiful view to the reading room, opposing the main entrance. And here as well, it's particularly delightful to see the many primary pupils run from one collection to the other, clad in colorful neon clothes. The neon is necessary so the little ones can be found should they get lost in the hustle and bustle of the city and brought back to the group of the same color.

Egyptian mummies

No other museum in the whole world can exhibit so many mummies. The plethora of Egyptian paintings is unique. The ivory statues from the Parthenon in Athens and the Erechteion were brought here illegally and through trickery. Greece is demanding they be given back so that they can once again be built into the historic temples from where Elgin has pried them out.

Cyrus Cylinder

On this, the great Persian leader had ordered to have the first ever human rights engraved in 1538 BC. He was also the one to allow the Jews to return to Jerusalem from their Babylonian captivity and to build the second temple.

His tomb has stood the test of time and can still be admired in Iran, which is the current name of the country formerly called Persia. The reason for the conservation of his tomb is that everyone respected him so much, even the subsequent conquerors, that none of them wanted to destroy it.

Buckingham Palace (4.4)

On our way to Cynthia's, we passed Buckingham Palace. As always, I'm impressed by its monumental façade and the broad street leading up to it, the Mall. At any time, the place is crawling with tourists who are watching the changing of the guard, which does seem out of place today, but is still an integral part of modern England's traditions.

Youthful folly

Long, long ago, when Charles bought his first camera, he and Cynthia decided to play a prank. The guards in their bearskin caps have to behave exactly according to protocol at all times. Cynthia was supposed to confuse them and Charles wanted to film that. So, she walked up to one of the guards and tickled his nose. The man in his bearskin cap kept standing up straight without moving a muscle, he was even able to keep a straight face. But just filming that was already a great success for Charles as a camera man.

The Queen's new residence

Queen Victoria was born in Kensington Palace and grew up there until her coronation. From then on, Buckingham Palace became the Royal Residence in London. If the flag is raised, it means that the Queen is present. In WWII, Buckingham Palace was hit seven times by German fighter pilots. One time, a British interceptor even collided with a German Dornier 17 and they both crashed into the castle's courtyard. This was actually captured on film and can be watched in the Imperial War Museum.

Revenge?

Did Hitler want to take revenge on the royal family? He had of course been informed that King Edward VIII had been forced to abdicate only because of his pro-German attitude and his refusal to wage war on Germany. His brother George VI on the other hand promoted a war against Germany in his first big address, The King's Speech.

The Queen Mum's reaction

She said: „I'm glad we've been bombed. This way, the people can see that they are not the only ones affected by the war – the royal family is not spared." After the first attacks on East End, meaning the docks and the homes of dockworkers, the Queen went down there to show her compassion towards the victims. However, she was booed. Through this, the people wanted to express that they thought the war to be pointless and unnecessary and that the public did not agree with the justification of the attack on Germany as the king had put it. In Germany, this kind of reaction had been counted on. But in times of war and under martial law, the protests of the public have no impact.

Departure

Officials wanted to protect the royal family and send the family members to live at Windsor Castle. The Queen Mum resisted. She said: "The princesses (Elisabeth and Margret) won't go without the queen. The queen won't leave the king. And the king will never leave." With this statement, she won much sympathy. The people honored the fact that she wanted to endure the dangers of the war just like London's general population, who couldn't leave.

Surprising

Along with the narrow-gauge motion film recorded by Wallis Simpson that shows Edward teaching his 5-year-old niece the Hitler salute, a picture has surfaced that Edward VIII had taken. It shows his sister-in-law and his brother with their two little girls and is dated two years later. By then, Elisabeth was 7 years old. It therefore had to be taken in 1935, shortly before Edward was to be crowned king for only 11 months. It shows Elisabeth, her hand sharply raised upward and, oh my, her mother right next to her – also doing the Hitler salute.

Eaton Square (4.5)

Cynthia's residence isn't far from Buckingham Palace. We were greeted cordially and I was introduced to Antonio, the senior chef of the Italian restaurant "Padella." He was there to feed us and had brought a cook and a waiter. Douglas was there already. He had brought Lizzy, his life partner. He had met her on a tour through America with a famous band. He was a drummer and had taken over for a sick band member. Lizzy was a singer in some of the songs.

Almost complete

Our dinner party consisted of 9 people, so we were almost equal to the 10 aristocrats from Florence in The Decameron. Another surprise was that Douglas had brought his guitar. We were going to sing old Italian songs they had sung when they had met Antonio in Italy. Youthful memories of Italy, evoked by music and food.

Battipaglia

The four-leaf clover had pitched their tents on the bay of Salerno one year after their vacation in Nice. Back then, it was a completely deserted beach, almost devoid of tourists. This is where they met Antonio, who was of the same age and later followed them to England, where he opened a restaurant. He was from Battipaglia, which had been destroyed by the Americans on their march from Sicily to Monte Cassino to Rome. Young Antonio had to evacuate to Naples with his mother, but later gladly returned to his old home, where he worked as a fisherman.

Strategy

Before Americans advance with their ground troops, they raze everything to the ground that could stand in their way. Their superior air force therefore makes it possible for them to minimize casualties among their own soldiers.

Tomato fields

Except for vast tomato fields, there was nothing upcountry from these broad sandy beaches. So at least the backpackers didn't have to buy tomatoes. The creepers of oblong Roma tomatoes were growing rampantly on the ground and were so full of fruit that the farmers couldn't possibly pick them all. However, there was no shopping facility close by, so the foursome befriended some fishermen, among them Antonio, who took their boats out into the sea. My friends were allowed to join them and the fishermen generously gave them fish they could roast on an open fire. One time, they even participated in a Mattanza. (If someone doesn't know what that is, they can simply google it.)

Capri

They sailed out into the sea in the West where the sun goes down and sinks into the sea near Capri. The first song that Douglas started to sing now, "When at evening the red sun sinks down into the sea near Capri, the fishermen sail out into the sea...". It turned out that Antonio could sing very well and even Lizzy chimed in, so, in the end, we had an orotund trio.

Sorrento

Fish and tomatoes alone weren't enough, of course, and so the four of them had to drive to Sorrento, which wasn't too far away. It's a small port town where tourists can cross over to Capri and then to the Blue Grotto of Capri. Once there, Cynthia put up her easel again and sold her paintings while Douglas played and sang for the people. This way, they earned enough money to buy wine, an absolute necessity, and of course grapes and bread and Parma ham.

Carpaccio

By then, the cook had prepared everything fresh in the kitchen and as an appetizer, he presented us with a wonderful veal carpaccio. The waiter was skillfully serving us and soon brought out a second appetizer. Spaghetti alle vongole, all dente. Nothing fancy, but to Antonio, it was most important to serve delicious food and he saw no point in elaborate garnishing.

Saltimbocca Romana

The main dish was also everyday food, but extraordinarily aromatic and unsurpassable in its taste. Along with that, we were served an assortment of various green salads, which were crisp and seasoned with the most exquisite olive oil and wine vinegar. Our dessert was freshly whisked Zabaione, as delicious as only Italians can make it.

After dinner

After we had eaten, the cook and the waiter, both of whom were Italian, joined us. Charles told us how they had explored the entire area back then. Right behind their tents, the famous temples of Paestum stood tall. The temple of Poseidon stood on a hill behind the beach. During the day, the four of them were having big swim contests. They wanted to swim out so far that they could see that temple from out in the water because of something Lord Byron had written. In his Italian diary, he recounted how he had swum out so far that he could see the temple from out in the water. However, the four of them discovered that this is completely impossible because of the curvature of the Earth. Obviously, Lord Byron had been grossly exaggerating once again to show off. He had actually seen the temple from the board of a ship.

Naples

There's a saying "See Naples and then you can die." Of course, this beautiful city was often the destination of their excursions, just like Vesuvius. Naturally, they also wanted to visit Pompeii. Cynthia knew most about it and was eagerly searching for the Villa dei Vettii. They finally found it. But to Cynthia's great disappointment, women weren't allowed to enter it. At least she got some kind of substitute with the sketches Charles made of the obscene frescoes and brought to her so that Cynthia could work on them. Her pictures actually sold better than Charles's sketches, they were more appealing. They sold particularly well with disappointed women who also weren't allowed to enter.

Today, this rule does of course no longer apply to women.

A rich American

An elderly American couple was interested in a fresco that Cynthia had painted in bold colors after Charles's draft. Their outfits already gave away that money was not an issue for them. The man was awed by Cynthia's painting and said that it would make a wonderful addition to the wall behind his desk. He asked the price and Cynthia, who was pretending to be Italian, wrote the amount of 1,000 lira on a piece of paper. Back then, one lira was worth about one penny, so this was a very modest price. However, you do have to keep in mind that at the time, money was worth about ten times more than it is today. Douglas, cheeky as always, said "That's in dollars." Now, the wife thought that this price was too high and she eloquently tried to discourage her husband from buying the fresco. But he was so taken with it that he actually paid the price in dollars.

Money Money Money

After telling this story, Douglas started to play the famous ABBA song with his guitar and everybody, even the cook and the waiter, sang along. That large sum financed the entire vacation of my London friends. They could now afford to drive to the Blue Grotto themselves and to Anacapri. They also explored the entire coast of Amalfi.

The joy of dancing

At night, they frequently went dancing or to the cinema. The most exciting thing back then was the neorealism of Rossellini. His movie "Stromboli," starring actress Ingrid Bergmann, was a huge hit. A boat trip to Stromboli and the Aeolian Islands had now become possible as well.

The biggest star back then was Sophia Loren. She actually comes from this area, from Pozzuoli, close to the Phlegraean Fields.

Mambo italiano

Douglas played the tune of this famous pop song and everybody joined him. We sang one song after the other, for example Felicita, Senza di te, Volare, Marina, Amore per sempre, l'Italiano and, of course, Laura non c'è. All these youthful memories turned our mood almost schmaltzy.

YouTube

And as if that wasn't enough, Cynthia then started to play the video of Sophia Loren on the big screen of her computer. We were so animated that we all started to dance the Mambo, unavoidably. We danced solo since there were only two women in our midst. The older people didn't dance quite as spellbindingly as Loren, who knows how to use her "fesses" like no other.

Not over yet

Guiseppe and Frederico, both of whom were good singers and dancers, would very much have liked to stay, but their shifts weren't over yet and they had to go back to the Padella.

La guerra parallela (4.6)

As a warm-up, Antonio told us about his childhood. His father was a Black Shirt. He was one of the camicie nere who helped the Duce (Mussolini) rise to power with the march on Rome in 1922. Later, he participated in almost all Italian battles against the Allies.

Declarations of war

Hitler's initial military success encouraged Mussolini to now declare war against England and France himself. He wanted to re-establish the "imperium romanum," starting in the Eastern Mediterranean area. First, his troops marched on the legendary land of Egypt with its historic reminiscence of Cesar and Cleopatra.

Suez Canal

Hitler was overjoyed that Italy had entered the war and promised right away to support the Duce with German troops. Should the Suez Canal become German property, England's shortest route to its Indian colony would be blocked. But Benito declined the offer. He wanted to be able to take full credit for his win by achieving it without anyone's help. He had only moderate success; the Italian troops couldn't advance to the Suez Canal because the English were bravely defending it.

War against France

Mussolini had declared war on and invaded that country just in time. Two days later, Général Pétain and Vichy-France surrendered. For quite some time, the Duce had been dreaming of reclaiming the Italian-speaking Riviera: Ventimiglia, Mentone, Monaco, and most of all, Nice. It's the capital of the great Italian freedom fighter Garibaldi.

Italian alpine villages

Italian mountain troops invaded all alpine villages where the population spoke Italian, from Aosta Valley to Mont Blanc. Soon after, Europe's highest mountain would no longer be known under its French name, instead, it was called Monte Bianco, the White Mountain.

Corsica

On this island, the people speak an Italian dialect, no doubt about it. Therefore, it belongs to Italy, even though Genoa had sold the island to the French king so they could repay their debts. This was shortly after Napoleon had been born there. And that's how he became a French emperor instead of an Italian freedom fighter.

Tunisia

Italy has a geographical and historical claim to this country. The Apennines continue through Sicily all the way to Tunisia. What's more, this is where the mighty Carthage was situated,

Rome's rival city. After England had snatched Egypt from the Ottoman Empire because of the profitable Suez Canal and the French had acquired the huge and rich territory of Algeria, it would rightfully have been Italy's turn to appropriate Tunisia as a colony. But the French coerced Italy to give up their claim so they could have Tunisia as well. Italy had to make do with Libya and back then, no one even suspected its oil wealth. Mussolini wanted to take advantage of the situation and rectify that decision.

Many possibilities

It was thrilling how many targets became available to the Duce and how many victories he wanted to secure in so many regions. Hitler only just managed to dissuade him from attacking Switzerland, where he wanted to reclaim Ticino, Locarno, Lugano, Chiasso, and Bellinzona.

Failure

None of Benito's military expeditions were successful. Even France, the defeated country, was superior to the Duce's Italian troops. And when English troops confronted the Italians in Tunisia, Mussolini couldn't help but accept German help. At first, this German support, led by General Rommel, who was called desert fox, achieved success.

Mare nostra

However, he just couldn't refrain from carrying out further attacks. The Adriatic Sea was supposed to become a pure Italian sea, a "Mare nostra." The sea was given this particular name by the Emperor Hadrian, whose leadership had led to the Roman Empire's biggest expansion.

A promise

In addition, Churchill had promised the Duce that he would grant him all coastal cities on the Dalmatian coast. The condition was that Mussolini manage to get neutral Italy involved in the war against the Danube Monarchy and the Emperor in Vienna. The Duce held up his end of the deal and Italy made enormous sacrifices in the battle of Isonzo and the struggles of the mountain troops at Pordoi Pass.

A broken promise

Churchill had to break this promise because he was obligated to give the entire coast to the Serbian king. His secret organization "the Black Hand" was supporting the assassins with money and weapons. Without his support, Gavrilo Princip wouldn't have been able to shoot the crown prince and his wife in Sarajevo on June 28, 1914. This was the starting shot for the glorious First World War that Churchill had been longing for for years. Therefore, the Serbian king had to be rewarded.

The Duce had to content himself with the Greek islands Santorin, Rhodes, and a right of occupation in western Turkey.

And at least he was given wonderful South Tyrol, where no Italians were living yet.

Albania

Benito didn't dare attack Yugoslavia, but in no time at all, he had taken control of the small country of Albania. And now he wanted to conquer Greece, which had, after all, been part of the Imperium Romanum in ancient times. However, he severely miscalculated the military force of the Greek troops and was badly defeated by President Metaxas. The Greek still celebrate their triumph on Ohi Day. Incidentally, Metaxas is, in fact, a member of the Metaxas family who produces the famous cognac.

An offer

Churchill immediately offered his help to the Greek president in his fight against the Duce. The president politely declined, pointing out that it wasn't necessary since the Italian troops had already retreated. Nonetheless, Churchill ordered English troops to land in Thessaloniki because he wanted to build a military base there in order to bombard Romanian oil fields. These oil fields were the only ones Hitler had access to and his only way of supplying fuel for his military vehicles.

An awkward mistake

Metaxas didn't want to let that happen. He wanted Greece to stay neutral and to not be drawn into this war, no matter what. And at that point, Metaxas's British personal physician made a truly awkward mistake. Instead of medicine, he gave his patient cyanide.

Some suspect that a connection between this mix-up and a phone call he had had with Churchill might not be out of the question.

Koryzis

Alexandros Koryzis was his successor. He rejected Hitler's demand on April 6, 1941 to expel the British from his country. That is why ten days later, German troops invaded Greece. Hitler didn't want to accept the fact that the English now had a military base that could sabotage his petroleum supply.

This quick reaction is quite astounding, seeing as Greece doesn't border on German territory. The troops had to march through Yugoslavia first, which wasn't on Germany's side, meaning they had to conquer it en passant. Or rather, they had to operate out of Bulgaria.

Suicide

As early as April 18, 1941, Koryzis saw no other solution but to take his own life. His successor, Emmanouil Tsondoros, was forced to flee after two days in office. He escaped to Crete, just like the English troops did. When German paratroopers landed on Crete on June 2, 1941, he had to continue his flight to England, passing through Egypt.

Memorandum

The war damages that the English had caused with their landing in Thessaloniki and later in Crete were supposed to be compensated for with reparations. In a memorandum between Tsondoros and the English ambassador, they agreed that after the war, Greece would receive the island Cyprus.

However, no one ever even mentioned that deal again after the war.

Lucky devil

The English landing in Thessaloniki was a disaster. Without even achieving any kind of military success, thousands died – from malaria. The British landing in Crete and their expulsion by German paratroopers was equated to Churchill's failures in Gallipoli during WWI.

The question arose whether he would have to resign. Through all the wrong decisions Churchill made – and they were the only kind of decision he ever made – he still always managed to stay on the winning side. From the beginning, he was always with the people who win no matter what – rich people.

A personal experience

I wanted to contribute a personal memory to the incidents surrounding Crete. The music teacher Mr. Vater came to our store and I got private recorder lessons from him, together with his daughter. She was as old as I was and we were both not going to school yet. One day, my music teacher came into the store, jubilant, and yelled: "Our paratroopers have landed in Crete." I never forgot this incident owing to the incredible news that Mr. Vater had to go to jail because of his happy announcement. Hitler had not yet released information about this landing since it had cost many lives. This meant that Mr. Vater had been listening to Radio London, which was strictly prohibited. However, he was a loyal party member and released after just three days.

Postponement

Antonio would have liked to tell us about the reconquest of Italy after the landing in Sicily. But it had already gotten quite late and so he postponed this part of the story. He promised he would invite us to his restaurant so he could pick up where he left off.

For tomorrow, we planned to meet at Douglas's in West End on Temple Street. He thanked Cynthia, our hostess, and admitted that only women know how to orchestrate such an opulent evening with a big banquet like that. Still, he revealed that he was also planning a "souper" at midnight and that, of course, his home wouldn't be lacking music and songs either.

The Fifth Day (5)

Due to our long evening at Cynthia's, we slept in. Instead of breakfast and lunch, we had brunch and our meeting wasn't until the afternoon. We were meeting in front of St. Paul's Cathedral.

Houston was waiting for me beside the entrance.

St. Paul´s (5.1)

This gigantic cathedral is almost as big as St. Peter's Basilica in Rome. It was built in 1666 in lieu of the cathedral that had been destroyed during the Great Fire. Lord Nelson's state funeral was in 1806. He was the winner of Trafalgar and is looking out over the city from his high seat on top of the pillar on Trafalgar Square.

In 1981, Diana and Charles's wedding was there, an event the whole world was watching. Its dome is 365 feet high, one foot for each day of the year. That's 111 meters. If you're feeling athletic, you can climb up 528 stairs and overlook the entire city from the top. The view of the dome from below is overwhelming. It's made even more impressive with magnifying glasses that let you perceive every detail. Many anecdotes are still told about the mysterious "Whispering Gallery." Unto this day, nobody knows why it was built.

Crypt

Beneath the cathedral lies a crypt that contains an uncountable number of tombs. Of course, Lord Nelson is buried there, but also William Turner, the great painter; the musician Sullivan; Fleming, who discovered Penicillin. Churchill is represented here with a monument, he isn't buried there. At least Florence Nightingale also has a monument dedicated to her here. She was the first to tend to wounded soldiers on the battlefields of the Crimean War.

Admiral David Beatty

Houston empathically pointed out his tomb. He was at the battle of Khartoum in Sudan, he participated in the Second Opium War. He was Churchill's secretary. He fought in the Boxer Rebellion in China, was admiral of the Royal Navy. In 1914, he took part in the battle of Heligoland and in 1915, he fought on the Dogger Bank. In 1916, he commanded the British fleet during the sea battle of Skagerrak. "Something seems to be wrong with our damned ships." But after that, he supposedly gave orders for military action: "don't forget that the enemy is a loathsome beast." Obviously, he had the same elocution as his former boss Churchill.

Reflection

Churchill also always stated that the Germans, whom he called the Huns, weren't humans but beasts. After 1945, this has been hammered into the Germans' conscience because of their prosecution of Jews. But how did Beatty already know that during the Imperial Era? That is a mystery still today. During that same battle of Skagerrak, the world's biggest fleet, the British fleet commanded by Beatty, was defeated by the Germans and most of their ships were sunk. More than 6,000 seamen went to their watery graves. The Germans also suffered great losses and almost 2,000 casualties. However, the British press presented this defeat as a big win.

I wonder how this battle would have gone if Churchill had still been chief commander. Due to the catastrophe at Gallipolli, he had been forced to resign and Beatty had become his successor. I'm guessing that the British losses would have been even greater.

Wren's tomb

Naturally, the architect's tomb can also be found in the crypt. A great polished plate made of black marble, no ornaments. And like at any other historic place, a teacher was sitting there with her young pupils. They were unconcernedly sitting on the gravestone or the floor in front of it and some were standing. The teacher showed them a big picture, illustrating what the cathedral had looked like before the Great Fire. This way, the little Londoners graphically learn about their city's and their country's history as early as elementary school.

City of London (5.2)

After our visit, we took advantage of the mild temperatures and strolled through the City of London. We climbed Ludgate Hill and after a side trip to the Old Bailey, arrived at Fleet Street, the newspaper street. Houston told me that he had also published some satirical material in the culture pages of some newspapers. Obviously, we also stopped at a few old pubs where we drank a beer each time.

Ye Olde Cock tavern

This cozy tavern had already been frequented by Tennyson and Samuel Pepys. That is where Houston told me at least one short joke. Churchill had been less than thrilled that the three Western occupation zones of Germany were uniting to become the Federal Republic of Germany. He wanted Germany to remain hacked in pieces forever. And when the Federal Armed Forces were founded even though Churchill had sworn that no German would ever again carry a weapon, his fury intensified to the point of bursting. However, as president, he was obligated to welcome the German chancellor, Dr. Adenauer, whether he liked it or not. During their first meeting, he was extremely cold towards Adenauer. However, by the second time, he had already accepted what had happened and was almost friendly.

Adenauer

Adenauer's statement "Why would I care about the rubbish I said yesterday" was an attitude even Churchill appreciated. He said "that could well have been one of mine." And Adenauer answered "the new Germany has mostly adapted to the practices of English democracy. If an important position in state is to be filled, it doesn't go to a party member anymore. Instead, the job is listed so we can find the most well-suited person for it. Following this principle, a well-paid government job in Bonn had been listed. Of the many applicants, three had made the shortlist: an elementary teacher, a merchant, and a Jew.

The most capable candidate

All three were asked the same question: What's 2 + 2? The teacher answered first and happily cried: "That's so easy, the answer is 4." The merchant answered: "It's not as easy as you think, but it should be something around 4." The Jew disagreed and said: "Of course it's easy. When you're buying, it's 3 and when you're selling, it's 5." Who do you think got the job?

Adenauer replied: „After giving it some serious consideration, I decided that my wife's cousin should get the job."

Churchill laughed and said: "I see. Germany really is on its way to becoming a true democracy, following its English role model."

Cheshire Cheese

After just a few steps, we were thirsty again and went to "Cheshire Cheese." They have real English goat's cheese there. It was Dickens and Chesterton's favorite pub. Surely some of you know Father Brown or the short stories Everlasting Man. In there, Houston wanted to tell me a story from his youth about FDR that he had experienced in Bad Nauheim where his parents were taking a cure. However, he decided to wait until later to tell me. He thought this president was completely uninformed and as unsuspecting as Adam had been before the Fall of Man.

But as soon as money came into play, he had brilliant ideas. When he became president in 1932, he passed a law that forbade people from privately owning gold. Whoever refused to sell their gold to a bank for paper dollars would be threatened with up to ten years in prison. Once 4.5 billion had been turned in, he reckoned that pretty much everything had been collected and the gold price was then increased by 100%. This way, the banks had cashed in 4.5 billion in one swoop.

To be more exact, the owners of those banks had cashed in. New York's biggest bank, the Chase Manhattan, belonged to Rockefeller and Baron von Rothschild owned several banks. It can be assumed that they reciprocated FDR's kind favor in some way.

Temple Bar Memorial

This memorial can be found in the middle of the road at the end of Fleet Street. It marks the end of the City of London. From there on out, Fleet Street turns into Strand and belongs to Westminster. Some interesting buildings can be found close by. We had a look at all of them, for example Temple Church, which was built in 1185 by the Knight Templars based on the model of the Holy Sepulchre Church in Jerusalem.

Middle Temple Hall

This is where Shakespeare's Twelfth Night was performed in 1602. All these buildings are located within a park-like green area that goes all the way to the River Thames. It's an oasis of tranquility with many benches for people to rest on. We sat down there and watched the ships glide by, illuminated because it had turned dark by then. Our walk to Temple Avenue, which is where Douglas lived, was a nice stroll of just a few steps.

Temple Avenue (5.3)

At Douglas's and Lizzy's

They were already expecting us. Lizzy was playing the piano. It soon turned out that she was not only a singer but an excellent pianist as well. She had an affinity to Jazz. Charles and Cynthia were standing next to her and listening rapturously.

Big salon

I was surprised by their lavishly furnished apartment. Douglas had always been one to understate. He liked to play the part of a destitute bohemian while in actual fact, he was part of the high nobility. Tonight was the first time I'd heard of that.

Surprise

He had prepared a big surprise for all of us. On a gigantic screen, he wanted to show us a short film that had even gotten an Oscar in 1933. He had therefore gathered our seats around the screen.

Pride of London

He wanted to kick off the evening without many words. But before he turned on the TV, we clinked glasses filled with the best English beer. It's brewed in London and only served there: Pride of London.

The Germans are seen as the world's biggest beer drinkers, but the Brits surpass them easily. Their beer and ale that go down like oil are beyond comparison. Even today, many English people still brew their own beer at home in buckets and tubs.

Announcement

The ladies joined us in our toast and Douglas announced that he had chosen this beer specifically because he and Lizzy would perform "Pride of London" to usher in the second part of the evening. By now, this song by Noel Coward has practically become a national anthem.

Short film

Without any further introduction, we all found a comfortable seat and he turned on the TV. He had the award-winning movie from 1933 on DVD. It shows the first time someone flew over Mount Everest in two Westland Wallaces.

The beginnings of aviation (5.4)

One of the two pilots, Douglas Douglas-Hamilton, 14th Duke of Hamilton, was his great-uncle. Back then, aviating was pioneering work. The second biplane was piloted by his friend and companion. Their photographers sat behind both of them. The extreme height, more than 8,848 meters above sea level, was what made this flight so challenging. That's about the same height modern passenger aircrafts have to reach in order to traverse the continents.

Glitches

During their first flight on April 3,1933, pretty much everything went wrong. Due to the extreme cold at this height, minus 40 degrees Celsius, the fuel froze, the air was too thin for a human being to breathe, and their oxygen masks didn't work because of the cold. The four of them were close to dying of asphyxiation. What's more, the cameras were blocked and the entire footage was useless.

Forbiddance

So, the four of them had indeed flown over Mount Everest, but without even one single picture to show for it. The London government forbade them from repeating the flight, deeming it too dangerous to their lives.

Tinkering about

The foursome was not daunted by this. They started tinkering with oxygen masks and cameras on their own. Back in the early days of aviation, pilots had to be able to take matters into their own hands. In spite of the official ban, they initiated a second attempt on April 19, 1933 – which was hugely successful.

High-definition pictures

This time, their footage was overwhelming. For the first time, people could see the immediate environment of this massive mountain, something no human being had ever seen before. The first ascent of Everest by Hillary and his Sherpa Tensing would never have been possible if Hillary hadn't been able to plan his route with help of these pictures.

Charles Lindbergh

The short film was followed by a general discussion. We all felt how incredibly exciting and interesting the beginnings of aviation are even today. Lizzy contributed a story about a fellow countryman of hers. He had been the first to solve the problem of long-distance flights by undertaking the first flight across the Atlantic, all on his own. She pointed out how those pioneers had risked their lives for their work.

International

These pioneers also kept in contact with each other across national borders. Lindbergh, for example, was a personal friend of Edward VIII, who was a fanatic aviator himself. For his inauguration after the death of his father, Edward flew from Sandhurst to London himself, a first-time event in the British royal family.

Night flight

Cynthia reminded us that back then, the problem of flying at night also had yet to be solved. Saint-Exupéry, one of her favorite authors, was also doing pioneer work in this field. She mentioned his famous book "Night Flight." He wanted to help establish a regular postal service between Santiago de Chile and Argentina. The height of the Andes was a further obstacle to be conquered. Since he had had to repair his own damaged plane lots of times, it had become something of an everyday occurrence to him. When he landed in the desert, all alone and without anyone to help him for miles around, he had to rely on his own technical skill. However, these incidents could also lead to chance meetings, like that with the Little Prince, that helped him through his plight.

A hobby of High Society

King George's younger brother, the 1st Duke of Kent, was a gifted pilot as well. During the war, he also flew bigger planes. He was my great-uncle's closest friend. The latter had even built his own runway on the hunting lodge of his family in Scotland, Dungavel Castle. His royal friend often landed there on weekends so they could compete with each other in air races.

It's the same runway that Heß would land on on May 10, 1941.

George, 1st Duke of Kent

He was the fourth son of George V and Queen Mary, the most elegant and extraordinarily beautiful Mary of Teck – she was said to be the most beautiful woman in all of Europe. Her son was a very handsome and athletic young man. To some, he was everybody's darling, just like red-haired Harry is today. To others, however, he was the "enfant terrible" of the royal family. He was the last one to marry a foreign aristocrat, Princess Marina of Greece and Denmark. Their wedding was celebrated pompously. All succeeding royal marriages were to British aristocrats or commoners.

Florence Mills

As a bachelor, he had had many love affairs with dancers, actresses, and singers. His affair with Florence Mills, the Queen of Jazz, caused a particularly big fuss. She is said to be the first really big black star. At the beginning of our evening, Lizzy had played us some music from her famous musical "Black Birds" on the piano.

Edyth Baker

Yes Sir, that's my baby,
You are my heart's delight,
Where is the rainbow,
Dancing till dawn

She was another one of the royal prince's lovers.

Noel Coward

Even after George had gotten married, he still maintained relations to other women and also – oh my – to dazzling Noel Coward. He was bisexual.

When popular actress Inge Meysel was encouraged to come out of the closet, she said, with typical Berlin bluntness: "I'm bisexual. That gives me the biggest selection." Evidently, this was also true for the 1st Duke of Kent.

Champagne

Douglas now switched to the second part of the evening. At the beginning of our evening, our topic had been the beginnings of aviation. The following subject was to be Heß's flight. This flight was one of the weirdest and most mysterious events of all during WWII. But first, we finished our beers and Lizzy had bottles of champagne served up. Up to then, the service personnel had stayed in the background, but now they brought out champagne flutes and bottles that were uncorked with loud pops. After we had said our Prosit, à votre santé, and cheerio, Douglas wanted to sing the famous London protest song by Noel Coward – "Pride of London." Coward had composed the song and written its lyrics after the most horrific air attack on London on May 10, 1941. 500 planes had dropped their bombs over the city, leading to most substantial damages. For want of an orchestra, Lizzy accompanied him on the piano.

Lyrics

London Pride has been handed down to us.
London Pride is a flower that's free.
London Pride means our own dear town to us,
And our pride it forever will be.

It's a declaration of love to the city of London.

Cockney feet mark the beat of history.
Every street pins a memory down.
Nothing ever can quite replace
The grace of London Town.

He invokes the city's historical importance.
Every Blitz, your resistance toughening,
From the Ritz to the Anchor and Crown,
Nothing ever could override
The pride of London Town.

Every attack does nothing but strengthen its resistance,
nothing will ever overpower London.

Melody

In the melody of the song, there's much to discover for music lovers. Coward supposedly incorporated sequences of other songs, from „God save the King" to "Land of Hope and Glory," even the German anthem "Deutschland, Deutschland über alles" (Germany above all else) seems to be included.

Rewrites

Following the horrific terrorist attacks of our days, many rewrites have seen the light of day that express the Londoners' resilience in this new and different situation.

His reason for choosing this song

Douglas explained that he had chosen this song to introduce our second topic of the evening because May 10, 1941, the day of the major attack on London, had also been the day that Heß took off on his mysterious flight.

Augsburg

For his long flight to Scotland, Heß had to have his sports plane completely refigured in Messerschmitt's factory. The kerosene in his tank wasn't even close to the quantity he needed for this distance. Instead of a second seat for a co-pilot and a third seat for another companion, huge reservoirs were built in that were supposed to last for the outbound flight. The plane would have to have been refilled for the return flight.

Start

As had been agreed on, Heß gave a messenger a letter for Hitler before lift-off, telling him that he was ready to take off and would now enter the plane.

Flight

He flew down the Rhine to Rotterdam and then across the canal. From there, he was flying low so the radar wouldn't register him. Since the air attack on London with 500 planes was starting at the same time, the British air defense was preoccupied with warding them off. As a consequence, the flight over the South of England wasn't very dangerous for Heß.

Plan

It got harder the closer he got to his destination in Scotland, Dungavel Castle. Churchill had been informed of his endeavor by the secret service. He also knew why it was taking place: he himself was to be deprived of his power and Heß was to appear in the English Parliament as a representative of Hitler. Heß was fluent in English and the plan was to have him negotiate a peace agreement between England and Germany.

After all, Churchill didn't have the best interest of the English people in mind, he only followed orders of American high finance. To be even clearer: his ordering party, Baron von Rothschild, is the number 1 in England and also in America. This party was to be eliminated by Heß's appearance.

Raid 42

In order to foil Hitler's plan, Churchill wanted to have Heß's plane shot down, nice and easy. With that, the whole thing would have been dealt with. Under the mission name Raid 42, 3 Spitfires and one special night fighter plane started hunting down the daring pilot. They had been informed that a German plane would approach Dungavel Castle and that it had to be shot down under all circumstances.

Confidential informant

Just as a precaution, Churchill had also planted one of his confidential informants in the group of high-ranking politicians that had gathered around Douglas Hamilton in Dungavel Castle. Should his pilots not succeed in shooting down Heß's Messerschmitt machine, this would still give him a chance to foil the plan.

Top performance

And, as a matter of fact, plan A did fail. Heß was able to escape all of his persecutors, in spite of the fact that he had no radio contact and was flying over a region he didn't know at all. He managed to find his destination even though a further complication arose: his plane wasn't specifically equipped for night flight.

Torches

The runway had been marked with torches so Heß would be able to land safely. Everyone was standing on the airfield and the plane was circling above the estate. Heß was already emitting his first radio signals to show that he was ready to land.

Alfred Horn

The code word that was supposed to bring him permission to land was Alfred Horn. This is how Heß introduced himself. Churchill had found a way to have his confidential informant be the one to take Heß's first message. The CI acted as his boss had told him. Instead of giving permission to land, he yelled "put out the torches, we have been betrayed!"

Bewildered

Heß kept circling over Dungavel Castle for quite a while, not knowing what was going on, until he started to run short on kerosene. Since it was dark and he couldn't see a place where he could land safely, he decided to jump with a parachute and let the plane crash.

The first parachute jump

Heß had never practiced jumping with a parachute, it was his very first jump. He had to take a leap in the dark. He couldn't see what lay beneath him or where he would land, maybe it would be in a tree or on a rooftop. It was the black of night. As a result, his landing was quite rough and he broke his leg.

Capture

Troops that Churchill had stationed around Dungavel Castle, so-called Home Guards, apprehended Heß and took him prisoner. News about his capture was immediately passed on to Churchill.

Oxford

At the time, Churchill was in Oxford. He wanted to wait and see how the representative's flight would go. In addition, he knew he was safe there since he had likewise heard about the simultaneous mass attack on London.

Satisfaction

Churchill rubbed his hands in glee. True, Heß hadn't died as he had planned, that might lead to some trouble down the road. But at least he was his prisoner now. He sat back, satisfied, and said he wanted to watch the end of his movie first – probably Casablanca starring Ingrid Bergmann. He would deal with the issue tomorrow.

Casablanca

Casablanca is a shrewdly produced propaganda film. It has cult status unto this very day. Back then, this Moroccan city was still under administration by the French Vichy-government. That is why the movie was exclusively shot in Hollywood. The famous café didn't even actually exist in Casablanca. By now, it has been built there, inspired by the film set, so that curious tourists can visit it.

Leak (5.7)

After Douglas had recounted the surrounding circumstances of this flight in a very exciting manner, we all wanted to know more. Where was the leak that had allowed the secret service to learn about his plans and foil them this way?

But first, we all had to top up our champagne and wash down the shock of this story with a big gulp.

Background

Douglas started to explain, warning us: for this, I have to digress a little. It all started in 1936 when the Olympic Games were in Berlin. Officially, this event was supposed to be boycotted. Only very few high-ranking politicians resisted and went anyway – simply because they loved sports so much. All the more as English athletes were participating as well. Cancelling the entire team's performance hadn't been accepted.

Special treatment

That is why these few high-ranking politicians were treated with the utmost respect by Hitler and his grandees. It goes without saying that Churchill did not attend the games.

Around the Zugspitze

Heß was particularly attentive towards my great-uncle, the 14th Duke of Hamilton. He knew that the latter had been the leading pilot during the first flight over Mount Everest. Heß himself was an excellent aviator who had won a prize twice during the flying competition "Around the Zugspitze." He had made second place once and then even first place. Based on this, the two practically became friends, especially seeing as communication was not a problem. Heß's English was flawless, as, incidentally, was his French and my great-uncle knew some German.

Appeasement

Neville Chamberlain, the one to sign the Munich Agreement, would have been ready to end the war after the coup of the generals around Canaris. He had been a picture of health when suddenly, he got stomach cramps and his personal physician told him he would die from terminal cancer within six months. This forced Hitler to go look for others with a desire for peace among the English government representatives. The pathological swashbuckler could not be allowed to keep the upper hand as a solitary tyrant.

Halifax

Hitler himself only knew one person, Halifax, with whom he thought he might be able to strike up a reasonable conversation. Shortly before the war broke out, he had invited him to his mountain estate and Halifax had made quite the impression on Hitler. He was foreign minister and in Hitler's eyes the most competent English politician of his time.

Narrow gauge motion film

There even are film recordings of their conversation. Eva Braun had filmed them. Since she officially was the assistant of court photographer Hoffman, state guests didn't notice when she was filming. However, these old recordings had no audio track yet.

Lip-reading

The recording was made in July/August of 1939, just a few weeks before the war with Poland in Gdansk. Their conversation was in German. And Halifax, who was one of the few people in on FDR's war preparations, revealed to Hitler how far the war industry in the USA had come by then. Hitler was horrified. It would be impossible to counter such an enormous armament potential. And it would come into play by 1942 at the latest.

We didn't know about all this until early 2017. Experts read it from Hitler's and Halifax's lips. It's not quite clear to which end Halifax gave Hitler this information. Maybe he wanted to advise him against starting a war with Poland. However, that would not have changed the fact that by 1942 at the latest, the US power elites wanted to start a war with Germany – they had, after all, been preparing it since 1932. This is called the "ten year rule," which is how long it takes to realize an armament of these proportions.

Heß's suggestion

Heß was Hitler's proxy, a minister without a particular division, a unique position. He had the power to sign contracts and his signature was as valid as Hitler's own. Now, he remembered how well he had gotten along with Lord Douglas-Hamilton, this great pioneer of aviation and one of the most influential people in English politics.

He also knew about the lord's friendship with King Edward VIII, another aviation enthusiast who had been forced to abdicate because of his sympathy towards Germany. Douglas-Hamilton was a good friend to his youngest brother, George, 1st Duke of Kent, as well, who, incidentally, was also a passionate pilot. What's more, Heß knew that the Duke of Hamilton hated Churchill and that in his opinion, Churchill was nothing but a henchman to the American high finance around Baruch and was ruining the British world empire.

Haushofer

Furthermore, Heß knew just who would be able to establish contact with Douglas-Hamilton: his secretary, Haushofer Jr. His father, Professor Haushofer, had connections in all capitals of the world. He was a professor at Munich University and had introduced a new subject: geopolitics.

Burckhardt

Burckhardt was the CEO of the Red Cross in Switzerland and had many contacts in the countries involved in the war despite the chaos of war. Since he was an old friend of Haushofer senior, he was willing to establish a contact between Heß and Douglas-Hamilton.

SIS associates

Neither Heß nor Haushofer were aware that an aid service like the Red Cross often has to work with the secret service of the country in question. This is how the entire exchange between Heß and Hamilton first came to the SIS. As CEO of the SIS, Churchill immediately realized that this was a plan to have him unseated. He disincorporated the respective department of the SIS, after which it answered to him alone. He set up its headquarters in the garden of his own private estate in Chartwell. He decided which information was to be passed on to the general SIS so the "conspirators" would have access to it. This way, the "putschists" never noticed that they had been betrayed.

Wrong theories

When it became obvious that Heß had been betrayed, the Germans thought they had found the culprit right away. Heß's secretary was Jewish (his mother was Jewish). He was held responsible for Churchill's knowledge of the plan and was arrested for it immediately.

Work permit

Heß was aware that his secretary was a Jew. However, he trusted him fully. He even personally made sure to get him a work permit for the job. His father was also beyond any suspicion. Heß had been one of his students; in fact, his favorite student, and the two of them had become lifelong friends. Any suspicion about Haushofer Jr. was surely not justified.

A problem

There was another problem with the whole thing. It could not be made public that a project co-designed by Hitler had failed. That just wouldn't go well with the Führer's "image." In the eyes of the public, the Führer had to seem incapable of making mistakes. This is why it was announced that Hitler had had no idea of his representative's scheme. Hitler said that Heß had acted this way due to his excessive pacifism and without the Führer's knowledge. The arrest of Haushofer Jr. was justified by claiming he hadn't alerted Hitler to his boss's intentions.

The English press (5.8)

Churchill announced to the press that there had been a struggle for power in Berlin and that Heß, fearing for his life, had fled to England to seek shelter.

The front page of one newspaper read "Brown parakeet on the loose," another wrote "The Führer's proxy has lost his mind."

Interrogations

All people present at Dungavel Castle at the planned time of the landing were, of course, interrogated. First of all the Duke himself, landlord of this castle, who had invited many guests. By the way, Dungavel Castle is not the family's main home but just a hunting lodge. Incidentally, Douglas-Hamilton has two titles and his main home is a palace so magnificent that it's easy to see how important a role he plays in Great Britain.

Defamation

Remember, Churchill was well informed about everything. It wasn't actually necessary to interrogate the Duke. The fact that Douglas-Hamilton denied knowing Heß at all was immediately recognized as an excuse by Churchill. But this lie just went so well with the story he had concocted. He passed it on to the press. Mentally confused Heß had imagined an agreement with the Duke, whom he had met in Berlin during the Olympic Games, and that he could convince him to make peace with Germany. However, the Duke supposedly had no recollection of this meeting and when Heß was presented to him in a lineup, he claimed to have never seen him before.

Expropriation

Churchill pretended to believe the Duke. But, of course, this betrayal could not go unpunished; however, the punishment could not be associated with the actual event. He also wanted to avoid inciting an internal struggle for power with this influential family right in the middle of a war.

It wasn't until 1947, years later, that their hunting lodge was legally taken from them under the pretense that it might become a pilgrimage site for English Nazi devotees. The family really struggled with this because many of their ancestors were buried in the estate park.

Infamous prison

The lovely country estate was turned into a prison of the worst possible kind. No other prison was the site of so many scandals. This was a calculated decision. The place's reputation was to be utterly destroyed.

Asylum camp

Lately, even that has been topped. Asylum seekers who are about to be deported are held captive there. Protests and counter-protests are continually alternating there. In the foreseeable future, the entire estate will be demolished.

James Douglas-Hamilton

He's one of the Duke's sons. He wrote a book that can be bought on Amazon. Its title: "The Truth About Rudolf Heß." I haven't read it, but it seems to me that he doesn't have anything new to report. He was probably urged to write it and confirm the widely known half-truths about what happened.

People suspect that there might still be some secrets that the public can't know about yet, seeing as all documents on Heß's flight are under seal until 2041. A 100-year non-disclosure is far from ordinary.

George, 1st Duke of Kent (5.9)

Churchill knew that the "putsch government" had planned for the king's youngest brother to become the future king. Edward VIII, after being forced to abdicate, saw no way of returning from his exile on the Bahamas to reclaim his crown in England, even though he would have been willing to do it.

During his interrogation, George stated that he often came together with his aviator friends on the estate because the runway allowed for quick visits. His lover at the time, Noel Coward, usually took part as well.

Churchill was satisfied by this excuse. It sounded very plausible. That meant that neither of these "guests" knew that Heß had been approaching.

Punishment

Nonetheless, Churchill wanted his punishment to be severe, especially since George, whom the people loved dearly, had been and still was a serious opponent, even after this failed attempt at taking over. So, the military secret service MI5 simply tampered with the motors of his plane when he and eight of his closest companions were deployed for a military mission. He was supposed to cross the Atlantic and fly to Newfoundland. Shortly after take-off, the Short Sunderland crashed, killing every person on board. Just an accident.

Widow

George's wife, Marina of Greece and Denmark, had blessed the Duke with a son just 8 weeks prior, a son that is still alive today. After the death of her husband, Churchill informed her that she would have to vacate her home, since only her husband, a member of the royal family, had been entitled to live there. Furthermore, she would no longer receive a yearly appanage to provide for herself and her children, since this also only applied to members of the royal family.

George V

He was the oldest brother and the father of the current Queen, Elisabeth. He took pity on the widow of his youngest brother and their three small children and took them in. He granted them some rooms in Kensington Palace. In addition, he used money from his private estate to provide her with some money so she could buy things for herself and her children. By right, Marina should have received a widow's pension, considering that her husband's "accident" had taken place during a military mission.

Rent

Later, when her kids had already become adults but didn't yet have their own source of income, they were still living in Kensington Palace. Then, a query was raised in Parliament, asking if they were contributing enough to the costs for the Palace's upkeep. While the Palace itself belongs to the king, the state still contributes to cover its expenses. The family's "rent" was deemed too cheap. They had to retroactively pay rent for all the years they had been living there, in addition to a fine. Since they weren't able to afford any of that, Elisabeth II, who had by then become queen, covered all of the costs for her relatives.

Disempowerment

It's not clear how exactly Churchill would have been disempowered. Was he supposed to be captured or simply outvoted in Parliament? After that last big air raid, the atmosphere in London had changed and everyone would have been more than happy to finally end this pointless and "unnecessary" war. Nobody believed Churchill anyway, he who was perpetually trying to heighten people's fears that their island would be invaded by the Germans, warning them: "defend the shores, defend your houses and gardens." What advantage would the Germans gain by occupying England? And what advantage would the English in turn gain by fighting the Germans? This war had been fought only on behalf of high finance in the USA. They wanted to crush Germany, this strong economic competitor. Particularly its export trade that did not flow through the world trade center in New York and whose transactions weren't in dollars.

Desire for peace

The prospective king wanted to support his people's desire for peace and grant it to them. His friend, Noel Coward, wanted to support him in his endeavor and prepare a peaceful atmosphere towards the Germans with his song "Don't Let's Be Beastly to the Germans." That's also the first line of the song. Now that the conspiracy behind it had been revealed, this could no longer be tolerated. The song was put on the "List of songs banned by the BBC!" and could not be publicly broadcast anymore.

Misconception

At first, the song was very popular. Even Churchill loved it; so much in fact that he apparently demanded several encores when the song was performed live. After all, in the song, the Germans are called "the rats" and in the last line, "the Huns," as they should be called officially. The line about Beethoven and Bach being worse than those "nasty Nazis," something like Jack the Ripper or Mack the Knife, was taken literally, not ironically.

Re-interpretation

However, now that Churchill knew that Coward had been involved in this attempt to end the war on Germany, he had to re-interpret the song. Now, the first line was already a scandal in itself and a provocation, seeing as it was meant literally. Coward really wanted to say that the English shouldn't be beastly to the Germans – at the time, this came close to high treason.

Noel Coward

After this, London's favorite entertainer had to accept that his concerts were being sabotaged. The press now gave him nothing but bad reviews. He was no longer booked for performances. He had become a persona non grata.

Today, his songs are no longer officially banned, but no one sings them anymore, it's as simple as that. It has become second nature to the English to be beastly to Germans. For emotional reasons, it's still impossible for them to sing "Don't let's be beastly to the Germans."

Performance

Defying the zeitgeist and the general atmosphere, maybe even defying political correctness, Douglas now started to sing, accompanied by Lizzy on the piano:

„Don't let's be beastly to the Germans"

Lyrics

Don't let's be beastly to the Germans
When our victory is ultimately won,
It was just those nasty Nazis who persuaded them to fight
And their Beethoven and Bach are really far worse than their
bite
Let's be meek to them
And turn the other cheek to them
And try to bring out their latent sense of fun.
Let's give them full air parity
And treat the rats with charity,
But don't let's be beastly to the Hun.

And I have to say, having all this background knowledge made this performance a really particular kind of enjoyment of art.

Delivery service

Just at the right moment, the doorbell rang and a delivery service brought our midnight dinner, le souper – perfect timing.

Sadly, there had been some trouble with the Hungarian cook. He had wanted to make goulash soup with bell peppers and pancakes with blueberries. So, Lizzy quickly switched to McDonald's. Hamburgers can be easily served, and they came fresh from a nearby store. To go with that, we all had a Guinness, even the ladies.

Speculation (5.10)

After dinner, we had a discussion. Our topic: What would be different today if the war had actually ended back then?

Indonesia

Would the Dutch still have the beautiful islands Sumatra, Java, Bali... and the Spice Islands? Back then, the Japanese hadn't yet occupied these islands. However, when they had to retreat in 1945, Sukarno didn't let the former colonial rulers back in. The Netherlands were so utterly destroyed and weakened after the Allies had landed in Normandy and fought battles on their land that they couldn't fight for their return.

Indochina

The same goes for Vietnam, Cambodia, Laos. At that point, in 1941, Indochina was still French territory under the Vichy-government. Later, they allowed the Japanese to conquer the land, who then occupied it until 1945. When the Japanese had to retreat in 1945, the natives didn't want the former French colonial leaders back. They also didn't want to be ruled by the Americans, who later staged an incident in the Gulf of Tongking in August of 1964 to create a pretense for marching on Vietnam.

India

Gandhi had already achieved a certain independence for India, but in 1947, India irrevocably became a sovereign country. However, India's struggle for independence would have surely gone differently without the military operations from late 1941 to 1951.

Africa

Belgian Congo, Kenya, Rhodesia... it all started to crumble. And those countries gained their independence. Just like Senegal, Nigeria, Cameroon... It took a while longer in Algeria, a country so important to France that it was even declared part of the motherland, giving the Algerians suffrage.

Certainty

Well, this was nothing but speculation, we all agreed on that. What's certain is that 6 weeks after Heß's flight, Hitler started his invasion of Russia, Operation Barbarossa. It's not quite clear how this invasion with no prior declaration of war is connected to Heß's flight. Was it planned in any case or did it only happen because the coup didn't work?

Catastrophe

What is clear however is that the decision to invade Russia ultimately led to the biggest disaster of the Second World War. To the terrible suffering of the Russian population, to the inhumane ordeals of the German soldiers, and to the atrocity called Holocaust or Shoa by the Jews. All of this began with Operation Barbarossa.

A final solution

In 1939, shortly after the Invasion of Poland, Hitler held a speech during which he declared: "If the Jewish high finance leads the world into a second world war, just like they did during the First World War, this won't be the end of the German people, but the end of Judaism in Europe."

His opinion was that the actual leaders of the USA were the big banks, meaning Rothschild, Rockefeller, Lehmann Brothers, Goldmann Sachs, Morgan-Stanley, Warburg, etc. Coincidentally, all of them were Jewish and that's why Hitler thought that the Jews were the true enemies of the German Reich.

The Heß problem

He hadn't died during the plane crash. Therefore, the parliamentarians and government members had a right to know what had actually happened here. Churchill had no choice but to let Heß be interrogated by a committee of inquiry.

His fear

He was very afraid that should the parliamentarians learn of Hitler's peace offer, they might be inclined to take it. He had already fended off three other big initiatives without revealing their content to the government members.

Pacelli

He was the Vatican's ambassador in Berlin. Later, he would become Pope Pius XII. "Hitler's Pope" as Churchill liked to call him. Pacelli assured the English government that Hitler would reinstate the status quo after the end of the war. That would mean that France would become independent again and keep its old borders, except for Alsace-Lorraine, which would stay German territory. Poland's old borders would likewise be reinstated. Only Gdansk, a city whose population was 98 % German, would be put under an independent German instead of a Polish administration. However, Pacelli could make no promises for the Polish territory that was currently occupied by the Russians.

King of Sweden

Sweden, a country that had stayed neutral during this English-German conflict, also tried to mediate, but without success.

Dahlerus, a great industrialist, launched his own initiative, authorized by the German big industry and also failed. Churchill thwarted each and every attempt to end the war because he had promised FDR to create the necessary conditions for a big war. And also because he was dependent on the financial support that he periodically received from Baruch.

Daily phone calls

He held daily contact to FDR from his "toilet" in the war rooms, something not even the members of his war cabinet sitting in the adjoining conference hall were aware of. There, he received his daily instructions, fresh from the American center of power. He knew that only the gigantic armament potential of the USA would be able to win this war. He also knew that each day, FDR was only waiting for a chance to enter the war. He only had to wait for the pacifism of the American people to be broken. And that's just what happened in 1941, six months after Heß's flight, when the Japanese attacked Pearl Harbor – apparently out of the blue.

Danger

But they weren't quite there yet when Heß was presented to the commission of inquiry. The details of his plan for peace couldn't become known yet. To prevent that from happening, Churchill had him pumped so full of drugs that he behaved like a madman, lost his memory, and could produce nothing but gibberish.

Result

The commission decided that it was dealing with a mentally ill man who could only utter incoherent nonsense, for example, that Germany wanted its colonies back. Furthermore, he carried no mission statement or mandate that would allow him to lead a negotiation. He had apparently flown to Dungavel Castle out of his own free will, without the Führer's or Douglas-Hamilton's knowledge and without any sense of direction.

Adaptation

This theory was eagerly adopted in Berlin. In a political sense, it would have been way more problematic to admit that a mission that had involved Hitler had failed than to concede that a minister had lost his mind.

Damage

Heß's externally inflicted drug frenzy went on for several days and led to permanent brain damage. Even years later, during the Nuremberg Trials, this was obvious by his insane look, the memory gaps, and his weird behavior.

Moments of sanity

Every now and then, Heß still had moments of sanity. Presumably, his drugs weren't administered all the time. During one of these moments, he wrote a letter to the English king.

His letter to the English king

He complains that mind-altering substances were being added to his food and that he was being forced to say things he didn't actually mean.

Scientific explanation

The letter was actually delivered to George VI, who then arranged a psychiatric evaluation for Heß. The psychiatrists concluded that Heß's suspicions were nothing but an autosuggestion of his psyche and that his accusations were completely unfounded.

Report

At the same time, the experts compiled a report on Heß's personality indicators. The scientists found that Heß was infantile and retarded in development. Furthermore, that his mental capabilities were extremely limited, you might even say that he was mentally retarded.

Remote diagnosis

The scientists took the opportunity to point out that his "boss" Hitler could be diagnosed in a very similar manner. Finally, the people had it in black and white and scientifically proven, the thing that everybody had been thinking all along: not one of the Nazis can even count to three. An authoritative result at last.

Fortune teller

According to the English press, Heß and Hitler had another little thing in common. Before take-off, Heß supposedly asked a fortune teller to reveal the perfect time to him. And many claim that Hitler also consulted with a fortune teller whenever he had to make a decision. I myself don't really believe that, but that's how the English newspapers presented it.

After Hitler had the genius Hanussen, a master of all trades, killed because he didn't always say what Hitler wanted to hear and also because he was Jewish, Hitler had to make do with an ordinary fortune teller.

Abracadabra

Apparently, Hitler consulted with this fortune teller before the big attack on London to learn the perfect timing – incidentally, this coincided with the time that had been revealed to Heß before his flight by his own fortune teller. However, this might just be another bit of fake news. Hitler told his fortune teller that he wanted to attack the city of London with 500 planes.

In trance, she said – when the moon is in the seventh house.

> I see 500 planes flying to London.
> And Jupiter aligns with Mars
> Over the water, over the canal
> Then hocus pocus oh oh oh

Well, what she's trying to say isn't quite clear, but apparently, to Hitler it seemed as though her statement could be taken as a good omen. And after his session, Hitler supposedly commanded that the attack take place.

Conclusion

Heß came to believe that with this unsuccessful confrontation with the parliamentarians, his mission had failed once and for all. Now, he wanted to take his own life. He wrote a suicide letter and jumped down the stairwell. His fall wasn't fatal, he was only severely injured.

Suicide letter

He did leave his suicide letter. He wanted "Ich hab's gewagt" (I took a risk) to be engraved on his tombstone. That's the first line of a poem by Ulrich von Hutten. With this, he wanted to express that with his flight, he had put all his eggs in one basket and even risked his own life. And that he didn't regret it, even though his plan had failed because of betrayal. His loyalty to his home country, protecting it from being destroyed, he thought those were his duties.

Ulrich von Hutten

Ich hab's gewagt mit Sinnen,
Und trag des noch kein Reu,
Konnt ich auch nicht gewinnen,
noch muss man spüren Treu.

I took a risk with all my senses
And so I stand without regrets
Even though I couldn't win
My loyalty can still be felt.

Classified information

All documents and protocols surrounding Heß's case are under seal until 2041. That's 100 years after the historic event. It's the longest time limit an event like that can have. There has to be something in there that the public still can't know about.

A practical explanation

All material that would incriminate Churchill has definitely, absolutely already been destroyed. They are keeping an empty case file under seal. This is due only to the idea that in 2041, the scandal of having documents destroyed will be much smaller. At that point, nobody but historians will even remember who Heß was. In contrast, nowadays there still are some people alive who remember this period during the Second World War.

Gratitude

Houston ended our evening by thanking Douglas and Lizzy. He announced that the next evening, the sixth one, would be concerned with the Russian Campaign. And to see us off nicely, another surprise was waiting for us.

Trumpet

Until then, Lizzy had presented herself as a pianist, but not as a singer. Now, to conclude our evening, she wanted to perform one of her favorite songs, "Summertime" by Ella Fitzgerald. An even bigger surprise was that Douglas was going to be accompanying her on the trumpet, just like Louis Armstrong had accompanied Fitzgerald. Even his closest friends hadn't known that he, a true musical genius, not only knew how to play the guitar and the drums, but also the trumpet.

The end of Part 1